I0564658

HOOD DRIVEN III

Loyalty Ain't Loyal Enough
A Crime Novel
By D Mack

Loyalty Ain't Loyal Enough

Deep-Street Publications
Detroit, MI 48227

Facebook: Hood Driven
Twitter: @HoodDriven
Instagram: @hooddrivenbook

Copyright © 2021
ISBN 978-0-578-91880-8
Cover Design: William C.
Printed in the United States of America

PLEASE DO NOT ATTEMPT ANY OF THE THINGS DEPICTED WITHIN THIS STORY …. THIS IS FOR ENTERTAINMENT PURPOSES ONLY.

By no means do I glorify violence. I just touch on reality the way it was revealed to me and so many others like me. It is what it is.

This book is dedicated to my baby girl Priya Mack. All my hard work is based on your future. You are my world princess, we got next.

Loyalty Ain't Loyal Enough

A wise man once said, never let your schooling get in the way of your education.

The drug activity in the Warren and Vandyke area was rampant this night. And everything seemed to be moving at a rushed pace. A small red blaze illuminated the face of Ray Ray as he pulled on the Newport from the shadows of the rented Nissan Maxima. His mind calculated every detail and he watched intently as the light-skinned mole-faced figure known as Brick, climbed from his triple black tricked-out Yukon Denali with his system thundering and rattlin' its parameters. His 24-inch Giovanni rims spinned to a slow stop as he shut off the engine and locked the doors with the press of a button, then approached the group of youngsta's who stood in front of the brown bricked tenement building talkin' shit and servin every fiend who walked up.

Brick collected small knots of money from all five of the rowdy looking youngsta's, then gave each of them a sack of cut-up cocaine and dapped them as he walked away. He made a gesture for the youngsta's to keep an eye on his truck while he made a run, then he jumped into the beat-up burgundy 87 cutlas and peeled off. The engine in the car was in perfect working condition, but a person wouldn't know it based on the appearance of the exterior. The rear bumper was bent, the bottom of each door had rust-holes in it, and the front grill was busted. There was absolutely nothing flashy about it, and as Ray Ray pulled off seconds behind it, he fully understood why.

He'd been following Brick for the past three months and had his routine down to a science. Brick always made major drop-offs to his connect once every two weeks. And it would always be done in the low-key cutlass to attract as little attention as possible. Brick moved a lot of weight throughout the city of Detroit, and had several clients in Cleveland, Indiana, Chicago, and Columbus. He was a real money-getter, and his suppliers loved his talent in that department. They would always look forward to seeing him on this particular night, because the rewards always seemed to be worth the risks. As Ray Ray followed him, he noticed some of the oncoming cars blink their headlights at Brick as an indication to kill his bright lights. But Brick ignored them and kept his lights on high beam.

Ray Ray gripped the steering wheel tightly with one hand, while he gripped the Baretta nine-millimeter with the other. Tonight, was the night that he would make his move on Brick. And it would happen in another five minutes when Brick would pull up in a Sunoco gas station like he always did, as a precaution to make sure he wasn't being followed.

Ray Ray began to close the three-car-length gap that he maintained the whole time, and became more anxious as he got closer… The police car that rode pass Brick suddenly bust a U-turn and sped back in his direction.

"Damn!" ranted Ray Ray as the police car zoomed around him and pulled Brick over. Ray Ray pulled over to a sound location and decided to wait and see what the outcome would be. He hoped they would just give him a citation and let him go on his way so he could proceed with the robbery.

The first thing the tall white officer noticed about Brick was the wine-colored birthmark on his forehead, identical to the one on the former soviet leader Mikhail Gorbachev, but he ignored it and started his line of questioning.

"Do you know why I stopped you?" he asked in a curious tone.

"Naw man, put me up on game." Said Brick sarcastically as he rubbed a hand across his shiny bald head.

"I stopped you because you had on your bright lights, impairing the vision of other drivers."

"Pst!" Brick sucked his teeth and turned his head irritably before responding.

"Man this raggedy ass car got all kinda' problems. The lights is stuck like that and I was gon' get it fixed the first thing in the morning."

"Oh yeah? Well that sounds like a good idea. Now let me see your license, registration, and proof of insurance."

"Pst! Damn man. Yall dudes been getting petty as hell lately." Brick grimaced as he aggressively handed the officer his phony license and matching registration. The officer took the information then went back to his squad car to check it out while his short black partner stood on the passenger side of Brick's car with his hand on his weapon...

Brick had been stopped several times pertaining to the bright lights, but it always worked to his advantage because the police would normally feel good about giving him a hundred- and fifty-dollar ticket and laugh to themselves about the beat-up condition of the vehicle. And even when they occasionally decided to search him and the car, the process would usually be brief, and he'd always make a successful drop...

Ten minutes later, the officer returned to the squad-car and handed Brick back his credentials along with a ticket in the amount of a hundred and fifty dollars.

"Preciate it officer, I'll holla."

"Whoa! Whoa!" squawked the officer as Brick attempted to pull off.

"Do you mind if my partner and I do a quick search of the vehicle?" Brick dropped his head in frustration and huffed before responding.

"Is that really necessary officer? Cause I'm in kind of a hurry."

"I understand where you're coming from guy, that's why I said a 'quick' search of the vehicle, so you can be on your way and we can be on ours."

Brick threw his hands up in disgusted resignation, then angrily opened the door and stepped his thin frame out with his hands held high.

Both officers instinctively reached for their weapons because of his sudden movement but didn't remove them from their holsters because of his visible hands elevated in the air.

The white officer quickly pat-searched Brick, grabbing his crotch roughly through the thin rust-colored Roca-wear sweat-pants. Then pointed to the curb and demanded him to sit down until they were through conducting their search.

While Brick sat there, he didn't sweat the situation at all. He just wished they'd hurry up so he could make the drop then hook up with a lil bad chick name Alicia that he met two days ago. He wanted to see what that small waiste and phat ass was made of. And he was almost certain that her thick brown lips would do some real justice to a hard dick.

Brick called out to one of the officers when he noticed him place his pack of newports on the roof of the car.

"Can I get one of my squares officers while yall doin' yall thang?"

The officer searched the pack again briefly before tossing it over to Brick with a lighter.

"Preciate it officer."

As Brick inhaled the smoke, he instantly felt better while he watched the officers rummage through the car. He smirked at how thorough they were in their search, but he still didn't sweat it because even the most thorough ones never found his stash.

The black officer suddenly held up his roca-wear jacket and blurted,

"Ay my man, why do this jacket smell like marijuana?"

Brick looked at him as if he was a dunce and replied,

"Cause I Smoked a blunt earlier today and I guess it over-rode my Hugo Boss cologne."

The officer didn't find the humor in Brick's answer and remained expressionless before he shot off another question.

"Well do you got some more weed?"

"Naw, but I got some more cologne." Brick answered sarcastically...

Five minutes later, a K-9-unit patrol car pulled up. They immediately let the Belgian Shepered sniff through the contours of the car. The hyper dog sniffed through the car at a fast pace as the officers hissed.

"Find it boy," in his ear and egged him on to find something.

After ten minutes of being inside the car, they popped the trunk and let the dog hop in. The K-9 sniffed around for about three minutes before he focused on one spot and started scratching aggressively at the floor.

The officers moved him out of the way, then began pulling up the bottom surface of the trunk.

After getting the second layer of padding removed, they noticed something green wrapped in plastic. They pulled, scraped, and brushed on the surface consistently until they finally had it clear enough to make out what it was.

12

The caucasion canine-officer ranted "Bingo!" ecstatically as his partner held the flashlight steady, and they focused on the substantial amount of money that was stuffed neatly in the man-made stash spot. They immediately placed handcuffs on Brick and placed him in the backseat of the squad-car...

"Damn," mumbled Ray Ray as he sat there and watched the officers pull hundreds of thousands of dollars from the stash and place it into boxes in neat thick stacks.

Ray Ray felt that the police had ruined a perfectly good score, and he was growing angrier and angrier with each passing second.

Brick sat in the backseat of the squad-car in a fit of quiet rage. He cursed to himself for being naïve enough to think he would keep getting pass that bright-light situation unscathed. Everything was going lovely, but now he had bigger problems. His boss Mr. Alverez would be pissed about the loss of the 1.2 million dollars, and it was never certain for one to say how the outcome would be.

Ray Ray's anger finally came to a head, and he didn't think twice about the decision he made as he looked himself over in the rearview mirror of the car. He rubbed a steady hand over his one-against-the-grain haircut and marveled at how much he resembled his late father as his brown lentil skin reflected back from the mirror. His neatly trimmed goatee gave his boyish facial features a coat of maturity that complimented his 5'9, 180lbs physically fit frame.

He slipped on a black ski-mask then slapped a 50-round clip into the Russian Kalashnikov AK-47 that previously sat on the backseat. He focused over at the officers again for a brief moment, then casually climbed from the car...

One of the three officers smiled at Brick as he taped up the last box of money.

"Ay Jenkins, I wonder what he was gonna do with all this fuckin cash." Said the tall white officer to his black partner.

"Ain't no tellin partner, let's ask him. Hey scumbag! What were you gonna do with all this dough?" he asked Brick through the partially open window.

"Buy Sushi muthafucka!" answered Brick sarcastically.

"Sushi my ass!" responded the black officer. "And for the record, I'm glad I could be the one to rain on your fuckin parade."

"Yeah Yeah, talk to yo partner or somethin man, cause I ain't got no mo' rap fa' yall hoes." Brick turned away as the smart-mouthed officers enjoyed rubbing the bust in his face...

A few moments later, as the three officers were making small talk amongst themselves, making rookie mistakes as they handled the money, the short white officer with control of the canine suddenly commanded the dog to attack the fast-approaching masked gunman.

Boh! Boh! Ray Ray dropped the dog with two sporadic shots, then swiftly subdued the tall white officer by planting the tip of the assault rifle against his head. He instantly swung the butt of the weapon into the officer's temple, which was just enough to produce a little blood-filled gash and drop him to his knees. A split-second later the weapon rested on the back of the officer's head again as the audacity of his brutal demonstration commanded the other officer's attention.

"A'ight listen up!" he yelled as his eyes shifted from one to the other in a calm controlled manner.

"The first thing I want yall muthafuckas to do is place those weapons on the ground, now. If I gotta say it twice, I'ma say it wit' two bullets to the back of his head. Feel me?"

The black officer quickly placed his weapon on the ground, then watched intently as the white canine officer focused on the dead dog with spasms of grief written across his face as he lowered his weapon as well.

"Put yall walkie-talkies on the ground too, then take all that money and put it back where yall got it from."

The officers looked dumbfounded for a moment, then slowly began doing as they were told. They were moving a little too slow for Ray Ray, so he aggressively nudged the subdued officer in the back of the head again and spat, "

Your co-workers must not like you, cause they gon' make me plug yo ass in about 30 seconds if they keep bullshitten tryin to use stall tactics –n-shit. Now tell'em to stop fuckin around and save yo life if they really give a fuck."

"Co- Come on guys, just do what he says alright, he's not playin." The officer pleaded with his comrades in a shaky tone. Then his two fellow officers speeded up the process dramatically and had the majority of the money back inside the cutlass within fifteen minutes.

Ray Ray knew the dispatcher would be calling back within the next 10 minutes, because it was standard procedure for them to check the status of active units every fifteen minutes...

Brick watched in awe as the scene that seemed to be straight out of a hollywood movie unfolded. He was so transfixed on the moment that he almost forgot what he needed to be doing. He shook it off, then worked his handcuffed hands underneath his hips where he was able to maneuver his body in a better fashion. He was now handcuffed to the front, and he planned to take full advantage of it.

He focused intently on the gunman again and watched every detail he could pick up from his demeanor. Brick had always been good at pulling the smallest details from people. If he couldn't see your face, he could remember other things. If he could see you in motion, he could pen-point your walk. Or pick out a minute scar on your hand that would slip past the average person.

He was very observant in a unique sort of way. But the highlight of his talent came whenever he was able to make direct eye contact with a person. He would remember them from anywhere from that day forward... Ray Ray constantly moved and barked a few more orders after the money was back inside the cutlas. And so far, Brick couldn't make out anything dinstinctive about him.

Ray Ray demanded the officers to lay face down on the ground and count to a hundred slow... They all complied, then Ray Ray didn't waste any time jumping in the cutlas cranking the engine to life.

Brick still didn't get what he was looking for as far as a description, and he knew it was now or never. "Tshh!" He used both feet to kick the window of the patrol car out, then quickly climbed out in a clumsy unsteady manner until he landed on his feet.

Ray Ray immediately looked back in his direction when he heard the shattering glass, and it was at that moment that they locked eyes... Time seemed as if it stood still in that instance as Brick stared pass the ski-mask into Ray Ray's cold and indifferent shark-like eyes.

An eerie chill ran through Brick's body as he held his stare for another five seconds, then broke-out running away from the scene in a zealous quick stride... Ray Ray didn't bother with trying to pursue him. He hit the gas hard and let the sound of screeching tires signify his departure.

He dialed the number to the rental car place as he blended into the night traffic and informed them on where they could find the rented Maxima. Then lit up a Newport, smiled to himself and mumbled-

"Today was a good day."

Chapter 2

After Brick safely made it out of the vacinity, he made his way back to the hood where one of his young cronies easily removed the handcuffs off with a hand-held blow torch. Brick came out of it with a minor burn on each wrist but was otherwise alright.

He dialed Mr. Alverez's number and gave him a brief rundown of what had taken place, then assured him he'd be at the rendezvous point within the next twenty minutes…. After hanging up with Mr. Alverez, Brick turned to one of his most trusted youngsta's who went by the name Tef. He strolled off to another room with him, leaving the other youngsta's in the living room of the chill-spot, playing play-station 3 and smoking potent ghanja.

He confidentially whispered a few brief instructions to Tef, then whizzed out the door seconds later in route to see Mr. Alverez.

Loyalty Ain't Loyal Enough

As Brick rode through the urban terrain in his Yukon, he couldn't help but to replay the night's main event over and over in his baffled mind. Brick without question was definitely of the gangsta element and had witnessed a lot in his twenty-seven years. But the way the gunman handled the entire robbery from start to finish, with a boldness he hadn't seen in years, aroused a touch of bizarre admiration in Brick for the stranger. Brick made a mental note that whoever dude was, he was a force to be reckoned with. And by the look in his eyes, the man had no phobias when it came to murder.

After 35 minutes of driving, Brick pulled up in the driveway of a beautiful five-bedroom brick home in Sterling Heights Michigan. It was one of Mr. Alverez's many homes that he used for business transactions, but it looked like the home of a plastic surgeon that was making an easy six-figure annual salary.

Two of Mr. Alverez's men greeted Brick at the door. They both were physically fit Spanish men wearing expensive Italian-made suits. They both wore stony expressions, and they never spoke as they pat-searched him a bit more thoroughly than the police had done earlier that night.

They instructed him to be seated until Mr. Alverez returned from private matters in another room, then posted up separately in neutral corners of the room.

A million different things ran through Brick's mind as he sat there awaiting Mr. Alverez's arrival. He hoped Mr. Alverez would be understanding about the loss, but in the same notion, he didn't want him to be too understanding. Because one of the key things he learned from being in the streets, was if a guy is a little overly understanding about issues that he would normally kill a man for, nine times outta ten, his understanding has already signed your death-warrant and he will rejoice the very moment the order is carried out.

Brick made a mental note of it and told himself he'd have to observe Mr. Alverez extremely close for anything that might not be in his favor... Ten minutes into his thoughts, the elderly Spanish man known as Mr. Alverez entered the room in a slow, hobbled stroll. The majority of his two-hundred-pound frame rested effortlessly against his triple-black marble cane with each step that he took. And his triple-black tailor-made Armani suit with matching square-toed Berluti shoes complimented his clean-shaven face and full head of wavy salt-n-pepper groomed hair. Even with the slight lean in Mr. Alverez's posture, he still stood a solid 6'1 in height. And even though he wasn't from an Italian descent, he still had a strong mafia presence about himself.

After being seated, he casually poured himself a shot of bourbon, then respectfully offered Brick a shot. Brick declined, then watched intently as Mr. Alverez downed his drink and gathered himself a few moments afterwards. Mr. Alverez showed no sign of anger, yet his demeanor was serious and firm. He placidly crossed one of his legs over the other, then fondled the expensive Perdoma Cuban cigar for a few more moments before finally breaking the lingered eerie silence.

"Brick, how long have you been working for me? He asked in a calm tone, already knowing the answer to his question. Brick cleared his throat before responding.

"About nine months Mr. A."

"And how many times have you witnessed me handle situations similar to the one that we've just encountered?

"A number of times Mr. A." Brick answered thinking to himself, (*Make ya fuckin' point dude, damn.*)

Mr. Alverez constantly fiddled with the unlit cigar during their discussion. And he hesitated on his next question purposely in an effort to display his patience. He always believed patience was the pilot of any conversation, and if it was applied effectively, it would always provide a beneficial resolution.

22

"Brick, in your opinion, would you say I've been fair in all, a few, or most of those cases?

Brick hesitated and hoped Mr. Alverez didn't notice the flushed expression on his face as the question he asked registered. He instantly thought about the time when lil Butch got robbed for fifty kilos and a half-a-million in cash. He didn't see Butch again after the meeting with Mr. Alverez until three months later... And when he did, Butch's appearance made Brick instantly tense-up in a servile manner... Butch had one eye, one ear, one hand, and a partial nose. And he was considered to be one of Mr. Alverez's best workers... Then there was another guy by the name of Lucky. He let a bitch name Syann set him up to get-got for 2.1 million in cash. He never showed up again after the meeting with Mr. Alverez. And on top of those situations, Brick thought about what Mr. Alverez supposedly did to his own baby brother. It was rumored that Mr. A personally cut his eyes out, and stitched them into the eye-sockets of a stuffed teddy-bear because he felt that his brother's character was soft and similar to a teddy-bear... Then he murdered him.

Brick thought about a countless number of other situations that turned out for the worst in regard to Mr. Alverez... But he wasn't about to arouse any aggression in him by telling him he was a cold-

23

blooded murdering bastard. So instead, he gave a more diplomatic answer.

"Mr. A, in my opinion, I feel that you've been fair in most cases. I guess we gotta' understand that this is the underworld we live in, and our method of handling our affairs is not always gonna' be understood to the people that's outside of our circle, or even the people that's inside our circle."

Mr. Alverez suddenly froze and averted his eyes from the cigar to Brick. He nodded his head in slow approval, then responded candidly.

"My friend, our world is definitely the underworld. And what is understood, has no need to be explained. And yes, you are a hundred percent right, it's not always easy to be a part of our system. And nomatter how hideous things may get, our methods of discipline are definitively the methods that our world calls for,"

He paused for a moment to let his statement sink in, then continued.

"Brick, I won't sit here and be dishonest with you about my feelings in this matter. I am extremely unhappy about the loss I've taken through you, mainly because I pegged you to be more responsible in your day-to-day activities. But what's done is done, and there's no need to dwell on a situation that can be rectified, so here's what I propose. You see this cigar?" He held up the Cuban cigar after asking the question.

"Yeah, I see it."

"Okay. Now do you know why it is unlit?"

"Naw...Why?"

"It's unlit because I don't believe in smoking a fine cigar outside the realm of celebration. And a celebration to me is whenever I make a substantial amount of money. Tonight I lost money, therefore, I won't be able to inhale the fine, soothing contents of the well-groomed tobacco... But, after I re-supply you tonight, and you come see me in approximately two weeks with a substantial amount of money, we will smoke this very cigar together. Are you game?"

"Of course, Mr. Alverez. I'm game."

"Okay, then it's settled. I want you to go with Ramo and he'll re-supply you tonight."

The Spanish man named Ramo stepped out of the neutral corner upon hearing his name and nodded in a friendly gesture toward Brick... Brick instantly got an eerie feeling from the highly tensed atmosphere. He didn't like the arrangement one bit. And on top of all the mafiosa talk, he felt that Mr. alverez handled the situation a bit too calmly, and that's what sent alarms ringing off in his head.

Ramo calmly strolled his six-foot four-hundred-and-fifty-pound frame toward the door and waited for Brick… Mr. Alverez stood up and held out his hand to Brick… Brick skeptically shook it, then walked pass Ramo with uneasiness dominating his demeanor.

As they approached Brick's truck, Ramo quickly spoke up.

"Follow me, I'm taking the Lincoln." Brick nodded in approval then climbed in his truck. He felt a slight sense of relief because the big burly Ramo wasn't all in his space anymore. He adjusted the steering wheel, then quickly lit a Newport.

After taking a few drags, he put the truck in drive. And just as he was about to pull off, the sudden knock on the window made him startlishly jump and drop his cigarette. It was Ramo. He urgently yelled

"Open the back door, I'm riding with you. And we will follow Ochoe in the Lincoln."

Brick quickly retrieved the lit cigarette before it burned a hole through his carpeted floor, then opened the front door for Ramo.

"I said open the back door Brick." Ramo yelled demandingly.

"Man what the fuck is wrong wit' da' front seat! huh?" Brick asked angrily.

"I don't like nobody sittin' behind me no fuckin' way." Clitzack!... The cocked chrone 45 that now rested on Brick's temple made him cease all movement.

"Open-the-Gah-damn-door, now muthafucka!" Ramo shouted fiercely as he pressed the weapon firmly against his head.

Brick felt defeated and sighed bitterly as he slowly reached down and hit the power-lock button to unlock the door. After hearing the click from the lock, Ramo opened the door and climbed inside.

"Drive!" he demanded.

"Drive where man?" asked Brick in an angered tone.

"Follow Ochoe in the Lincoln."

Brick breathed a heavy sigh again out of frustration, then abruptly pulled off...

After ten minutes of driving to a destination unknown to Brick, his thoughts were now on full throttle.

The Lincoln finally slowed down by a narrow, secluded alleyway. Ochoe slowly turned left into it and cruised slowly into the darkness until he was satisfactorily out of sight.

He killed the headlights, and the black Lincoln seemed as if it suddenly vanished into the quiet, desolate darkness... When Brick saw this, he instantly went into panick mode. He abruptly averted his eyes to the lights he watched in the rearview mirror, then nervously contemplated his next move...

"Fuck this!" he mumbled. Then without a second thought, he slammed on the brakes and frantically leaped out of the truck... Boh! Boh! Boh! ...Ramo instantly fired shots at Brick from the backseat as the truck began to slowly roll again... Brick ducked and ran toward the lights he'd been watching in his rearview as Ramo sprung from the rolling truck blastin' fiercely at him.

Suddenly, rapid gunfire zoomed pass Brick as the figure he ran toward trotted in his direction with guns blazin. When they finally came face to face, Tef handed Brick a 45 Desert Eagle, then resumed firing at Ramo with the semi-automatic MP-5.

Ramo quickly turned his big frame around and attempted to get out of harm's way but was hastily spent back toward Brick and Tef as the bullets they discharged tore into him with vicious thuds. He stumbled backwards and fired wild shots as Brick's truck finally crashed lightly into a non-working alley pole.

Brick signaled for Tef to go after Ochoe while he aggressively continued to converge on Ramo. He had no intentions of letting Ramo get away, because he knew that Ramo would've humiliated him before killing him. It was often rumored in the streets that Ramo went both ways, and would normally make his victim suck his dick, or sodomize them before killing them. For this reason alone, Brick hated him even more and used this as his motivation to successfully eliminate him… Ramo stumbled several times from the rapid loss of blood and continued to let off reckless shots until his weapon was empty. Brick smiled to himself as he quickly ran up on him. Boh! "Aahhg!" Brick put a bullet in his left knee-cap. Boh! Then put one in his right knee-cap.

Ramo dropped to the ground and howled out in agonizing pain.

"Manicong! Puta! Puta!" He shouted foul obscenities to Brick in spanish as he panted and attempted to drag himself away from his attacker.

Brick enjoyed the scene and smiled at the fact that Ramo's efforts were all in vain. Boh! Brick let off another shot. This time ripping through Ramo's mid-abdominal section, instantly causing him to have an unexpected bowel movement. Ramo aggressively clutched his stomach and tried desperately to catch the eluded breath that was knocked out of him from the impact of the new slug.

Brick knew he was suffering and loved every second of it. He stood over Ramo with a devilish grin and spat,

"If yo' slimy ass get re-incarnated, tell ya bitch-ass boss Mr. Alverez he fucked wit' the wrong nigga this time. And as for you, I want you to know that I enjoyed bein' the nigga who slumped yo faggot ass, poppi!"

Ramo released a sickening cough, then smiled through bloody lips as he slid his hand down to his crotch and mumbled,

"I would've truly enjoyed you baby." Then laughed to the top of his lungs as he squoze his meat in a sexual manner and awaited the fate that he knew was inevitable.

Brick irately leaned forward and slapped him hard across the face with the gun, then reached inside his slacks and gripped his dickhead... He pulled his dick to it's exceeded limitations and slightly beyond, causing Ramo to cry out and reach for Brick's hand. Boh!

"Aahggg!" Brick shot him in the hand, then placed the barrel against his outstretched penis and snarled,

"You probably woulda' had fun wit' me bitch. But not as much fun as this." Boh! The bullet tore a chunk of the soft gristle from his member, leaving it attached by only a thin portion of cartilage and skin.

Brick continued to pull, keeping it stretched as he placed the gun on the remaining portion. Boh! This time the bottom half dropped, and the head remained in Brick's hand... Ramo's pure-shock facial expression was straight out of a horror movie. His eyes were bucked, and his mouth was wide open, stuck in a silent scream.

Brick pushed the half-a-dolla sized penis-head into his open mouth, then pushed it closed from the bottom of his chin. Ramo suddenly snapped out of his daze and fought desperately to open his mouth as Brick forcibly held it shut. A few moments later, the regurgitated blood from Ramo's internal bleeding filled his mouth and pushed its way out the corners of his lips... Ramo struggled even more as he found himself taking deep swallows in an effort to relieve his blood-filled mouth... Suddenly, his eyes bucked even wider as he felt the lump of his own flesh slide down his throat.

Brick also noticed the moment he swallowed it, which was the moment he released him and laughed at the anguished look on his face.

"Now that's what I call givin' good head." He stood over the humiliated pain stricken Ramo chuckling and taunting him some more before he finally retorted,

"It's been real playboy, kiss dat ass goodbye." He aimed the gun between Ramo's eyes and mouthed "Bang" without pulling the trigger, then squawked,

"Die slow muthafucka, you earned it."

Ramo looked as if he wanted to cry a million tears. The disappointment he felt had him suicidal at the least. He wished to God that he had extra ammo in his weapon so he could make it all go away with one pull of the trigger. But it was all just wishful thinking, and he felt totally disgraced as he watched Brick walk away without putting him out of his misery.

As Brick advanced toward Tef in the darkness of the alley, he suddenly heard two loud pops that coincided with the two sudden flashes of light he saw...

When he got closer, he saw Tef standing over Ochoe's corpse that sported two bullet holes in the center of his forehead.

Tef's dark skin, thin frame, and short dreads added an eerie look to his already menacing appearance as he stood there.

Brick had a premonition that Mr. Alverez was going to order a hit on him once he informed him about the stolen money, so he took prior precautions and told Tef to follow him to the location and jump out blastin' the very second he noticed any false moves. And like always, Tef came through like the trooper he was.

Tef was a young 18-year-old with a heart of stone, originally from the Calliope Projects in New Orleans. He ended up in Detroit in tow with his mother and little sister due to the hurricane Katrina disaster.

He met Brick at a local car wash that he'd gained employment at, and Brick instantly took a liking to him and put him under his wing after witnessing him slap around the arab who owned the spot. The arab tried to play Tef like a buster and hold back on his checks because of his geographic status, but Tef wasn't buyin it... The day that it finally came to a head, Tef viciously stomped the arab out, then angrily asked Brick if he was strapped? Brick smiled and handed Tef a black snub-nosed 44 bulldog revolver with no hesitation. He got a real kick out of watching Tef fearlessly aim the gun at the man's head and squeeze the trigger at least four times before realizing the gun had no bullets in it.

Another thing Brick liked about Tef was that he didn't smoke weed or drink alcohol. He was just a natural-born hustler who loved to play Madden, drink apple-juice, and would murder at the drop of a dime... He was Brick's best kept secret.

Brick and Tef quickly fled the scene as they heard police sirens in the distance. Meanwhile, Mr. Alverez sat in a comfortable Italian-crafted leather recliner puffin on the expensive cigar with a devilish smirk on his face.

He'd lit up five minutes after Brick left with Ramo and Ochoe, but little did he know, his celebration was premature. Ochoe was now in the morgue with two holes lodged in his skull, and Ramo died on the operating table while the medical technicians attempted to retrieve his penis from his stomach. He was so fervid on getting his dick cut from his stomach, he never even mentioned who it was that mangled him.

Chapter 3

Ray Ray smiled to himself after he stashed his new fortune in one of his safe houses, then drove non-stop to his main house in the Boston Edison District. After pulling into his circular driveway, he was greeted by his two little girls Myonly and Love, along with his son lil Ray. The warm hug that he gave all three of them caused him to slip into a brief state of past and present reflection. He wondered how long it would be before his complicated predicament would shatter his dreams of living a worry-free life and afford him the priviledge of watching his children grow up to be productive citizens, which was a far cry from what he, his wife Sheila, and lil Ray's mother Syann was. He and Sheila were both fugitives who'd committed murder more than once, and It was safe to assume that they would both die in prison if they were ever captured. Syann was already in federal prison doin' a ten-year bid. And even though the charges was trumped up because of the fact that she wouldn't rat-out Ray Ray. She still got a slap on the wrist considering all the things that she didn't get arrested for.

Old memories continued to flood Ray Ray's mind as he thought about how he grew up hating all drug dealers after witnessing his parents and close friend get murdered by neighborhood drug dealers. He has and always will attribute his relentless spree of murder and mayhem to the unmerciful, horrific day in question. And whatever was turned on inside of him that day, created a man that is today feared by most, hated by many, and loved by few. Ray Ray lost certain friends that he considered family and accumulated a countless number of enemies. He often struggles with the stability of his conscienceness while reflecting on all the stress and fear that he caused his wife and children. And sometimes he still can't believe how he was eventually able to tap into an effective source that enabled him to successfully extract his woman from prison on a thirty-year sentence for a murder she commited to save his life... Then on top of all that, his two little angels ended up being kidnapped by a low-life Mexican who felt it'd be a good idea to extort him... Street wars immediately ensued afterwards, and soul after soul became more consumed by the grasps of the trenches. The bloodshed seemed never-ending, and the fumes of cordite and gunpowder was the dominant odor that lingered throughout the hood. Ray Ray had more than enough money to leave the country and start a new life like he once did before. But it always seemed as if some unseen force had a firm grip on his heart. And nomatter where he went, or how much his mind wrestled with logic, some part of his dark past would either find him, or he would always find a relevant excuse to come back to so-call end the game... When in all actuality, it was really to play the game... And play it hard.

Chapter 4

As ex-officer Smitty Branch sat attentively in the open-court hearing of a Duty-Reinstatement deposition on his behalf, he felt slightly agitated by the constant stares he received from a few of the female attendees in the room. They occasionally whispered among themselves about the gruesome appearance of Smitty's 85 percent charred face and head. The third-degree burns that claimed a once-upon-a-time handsome face made Smitty resent his every trip to the bathroom mirror. He hated the permanent mask that would undoubtedly go to the grave with him, re-shaping his identity for the pure adornment of public display. After five surgeries and a heep of medical expenses, Smitty was more than eager to regain his position as a Detroit police officer. He ultimately felt that it would be his best chance at someday getting revenge on the person responsible for the now primary insecurity in his life, as well as bleed the streets for all the monetary opportunities available. As the proceedings went forward, Smitty reflected on the spark of events that all led up to his present circumstance, as the opposing caucasion-female state representative argued diligently against his re-instatement... *The memories of how the feds moved in on him and busted up his illegal string of activities danced in his head and caused him to feel a bit grief-stricken from the sudden hault in his game. He loved what he was doing in the streets and had no remorse for whoever became victimized by his corrupt ways. He was literally a middle-aged black criminal with a badge. And was known in the hood for doing whatever any street dude would do, including murder. Smitty had assisted a lot of thorough street individuals on certain capers, but in his opinion, Ray Ray was by far one of the most notorious dudes he'd ever assisted. He reflected on how he aided Ray Ray in the cold-blooded murder of an FBI agent named Nathaniel Lawson, a-k-a Boon. Then later ratted him out to the feds when the heat finally came down on him for unrelated crimes. Smitty felt that it was so ironic how Ray Ray ended up catching up with him through dealing with Syann and seized the opportunity to not only attempt to murder him but torture him by dowsing his head with lighter fluid, then cruelly setting it ablaze.... Smitty barely escaped with his life. And from that point forward, he vowed to do whatever it took to get some payback on Ray Ray.*

Smitty's body tensed up and knots formed in his stomach when he heard the state representative continue to speak negatively against him. Federal Agent E. Burns leaned toward Smitty upon recognizing his discomfort and whispered.

"Calm down man, nomatter what she says, I got you. You stuck to your end of the bargain, and we'll stick to ours." Smitty relaxed a little after hearing what agent Burns had to say, then briefly recollected the proposal the feds had brought to him. *They assured him that they would get him reinstated as a police officer for his effort in helping them capture Ray Ray, as well as set up a few drug dealers for them. Which he happily agreed to do both.*

The state attorney called the chief of police to the stand, then cleared her throat before proceeding.

"Hello chief Dunkin, how are you today?"

"I'm fine, thank you." Answered the black pot-bellied middle-aged chief.

"Chief, I'd like to ask you a few questions about one of your former employees. A Mr. Smitty Branch." A gleam from the center of the chief's receeded head glimmered towards the onlookers as he nodded in approval of her question to him.

"Ok chief, in all of your years on the force with Mr. Branch, what would be a fair assessment of his character as an officer?"

"Well, I'd have to say that Smitty was a good officer. And when the charges against him from the government surfaced, I myself was personally shocked by what he was being accused of."

"Shocked, chief Dunkin?"

"Yes, shocked."

"Chief Dunkin. The red folder that I have here in my hands contains the initial report and statements you gave when his indictment on federal charges was first brought to light. So before we proceed any further, do you still feel that Mr. Branch's conduct was, *'and I quote'* A shock to your department?" Chief Dunkin cleared his throat before responding.

"Mrs. Drew, it goes without saying that no branch of law enforcement ever expects allegations of this magnitude to surface regarding any of their employees. But I think it's imperative that we remind ourselves of the essential phrase in its entirety of the situation, (*Allegations.*) So, in regard to your question Mrs. Drew, I think my initial term was in fact the appropriate one. I was shocked to hear about the allegations in reference to officer Smitty Branch."

Mrs. Drew swiftly opened the folder then took a few slow steps towards him as she processed the information silently. She looked up at chief Dunkin with the folder still open, then proceeded.

"Okay chief Dunkin, right here it says in this report, and once again I quote, *'We have suspected officer Branch of wrongdoing in the past, which brought us to conduct an internal investigation on him to make sure his conduct was in fact in accordance with the policies and statues of our establishment. And during that investigation, we discovered unlawful activities that would give significant validity to the new allegations that the government has brought against officer Branch. And we'd like to make it clear that we will fully co'operate with the government in their effort to get to the bottom of the situation and bring justice to the forefront.'*

"Chief Dunkin do you remember making that statement?" Chief Dunkin glanced over the room uncomfortably before responding.

"Mrs. Drew with all due respect, we are not on trial here. This is simply a reinstatement hearing. And yes, I do remember making that statement. I'm a man that's never had a problem admitting when I'm wrong. And at that particular time, my judgement in the matter was not accurate."

"Chief Dunkin, you weren't speaking in those statements based on your judgement. You were speaking based on factual evidence and you know it."

"Mrs. Drew," Chief Dunkin interjected in an irritable manner.

"Do you have something personal against Mr. Branch?"

"No I do not!" She answered angrily.

"Well what is your problem?"

"My problem is the fact that Mr. Branch's criminal history reflects an assortment of assaults, robberies, narcotics, and firearms violations. And it's truly appauling to me that we are willing to ignore that unruly part of his life and send him back out in our society to so-call protect and serve our citizens. There's something seriously wrong with this picture don't you think." She abruptly turned toward Smitty Branch after her statement.

"And isn't it true Mr. Branch that you were also indicted on civil rights charges for brutally beating a man up before you lost your badge?"

Smitty was shocked that she brought that up too, but he kept a straight face and didn't say a word. One of the caucasion males from the three-judge panel spoke up.

"Alright Mrs. Drew, I think you've fully made your point here today. So that'll be all for now. We will recess this hearing and return with our decision in one hour...

During the recess, Smitty approached chief Dunkin in the lobby and offered his hand as a gesture of appreciation for speaking in his favor. But chief Dunkin just looked at it as if it was poison, then attempted to walk away.

"Hold up chief, we don't have to conduct ourselves in this manner. I just wanted to thank you for your support in times like this." Chief Dunkin grimaced before responding.

"Look man, don't patronize me, alright. Cause you know how I really feel about you despite all that bullshit I said in your favor on the stand. So don't thank me, thank him." He pointed at agent Burns aggressively then walked away.

Agent Burns casually approached Smitty and smirked sarcastically as he watched chief Dunkin scurry away with an expression of disgust clearly evident on his face. Agent Burns held fast on his smirk as he thought about how stubborn chief Dunkin was in the beginning. That is until he disclosed all the evidence to him about the stolen funds from the confiscation-department. *Chief Dunkin had been stealing money from the police department for years. And the feds were about to indict him until they realized they could use his assistance in issues such as this. So they held the indictment off until they would get an answer from him. And once the chief finally saw the evidence against him, he spared himself the embarrassment and went along with their program...*

After the 60-minute recess was over, Smitty Branch and Agent Burns were all smiles when the court announced the decision in Smitty's favor. Smitty was officially a police officer again, and the state representative Mrs. Drew was more than unhappy with the outcome... And before the courts disbursed, she aggressively approached Smitty and spoke in an icy tone.

"Congratulations on your victory Mr. Branch. But now I'm gonna need you to sign a waiver of liability, absolving the justice department of any responsibility for your well-being." She handed him a pen along with a waiver form, but agent Burns stepped up irately before he could sign it.

"Come on woman, what's your problem?"

"I thought you would've figured that out by now agent Burns." She scolded.

"Now either he signs it, or I push for a speedy appeal and we do this thing all over again next month. Same time, same place. Your call." Agent Burns shot daggers at her with a cold stare. Then reluctantly nodded for Smitty to sign it so they could put the situation behind them and move forward.

After Smitty signed, Mrs. Drew sarcastically spat,

"Oh, and officer Branch, don't think for one second your reinstatement gives you the right to abuse your authority. So please keep in mind that your conduct will be closely monitored by myself, and others who share my interest in matters like such, I promise." She winked then pranced away switching her petite ass in a skank, diva-like manner.

"Man you should've fucked that evil red-head bitch agent Burns. Maybe then she would've considered us a friend instead of a foe." Agent Burns chuckled at Smitty's comment then turned and headed toward the exit.

Chapter 5

Shortly after Brick and Tef made it back to their safe house, Brick called an emergency meeting with his fifteen workers that were all within the age-range of seventeen to twenty-five.   He briefly explained about his new beef with Mr. Alverez, leaving out the details of what started it as well as the murders that took place because of it. He let them know that their turf would be extremely dangerous within the next couple weeks. And advised everyone to take extra safety precautions in every move they made.

Brick knew that his crew would run through the fifteen keys of coke that he had left, in a matter of a couple weeks. And that's only because he wouldn't let them sell it all in weight. It would be broke down to ounces and rocks because he figured this would buy him some time to find a new connect. Brick had always kept some extra coke put back in case something like this ever occurred.

And although he knew he had enough clientale to sell it all by himself, his main concern in times like this was to make sure his crew was still eating, so he distributed it all out to them. After the meeting was adjourned and all the team-players disbursed, the call from Mr. Alverez came in on Brick's cellphone. Brick gave Tef a heads-up look before answering, then he answered.

"Hello."

"Hello Brick." Mr. Alverez spoke in a calm, yet angered tone.

"Brick..Brick..Brick. I just called to share some factual information with you my friend."

"And what factual information might that be Mr. A?" Brick asked sarcastically.

Mr. A exhaled a misty cloud of cigar smoke before he continued.

"Brick, in my profession, sometimes ignorance can be forgiven. But stupidity, I can never seem to forgive." He paused momentarily to let his statement sink in, then continued.

"It was stupid to assassinate Ochoe and Ramo, Brick. Very stupid."

"Yeah? Well it was stupid for you to order them taco eatin' muthafuckas to kill me. So fuck Ochoe and Ramo, Mr. Alverez. The tables turned and I'm here, they not." Mr. Alverez paused again in an effort to let his anger subside, then spoke emphatically.

"Brick, I have a brand new freshly imported victory cigar with your name on it, and-" Brick angrily cut him off.

"Let me tell you somethin' you fake-ass Capone. Fuck you and that bitch-ass cigar, and when you come, you betta come right!" –Click!... Brick hung up on him, then turned toward Tef and squawked,

"Man that old bastard got a lot of fuckin' nerves. Callin me with that fake ass Gotti shit. Brick's phone rang again just as he completed his sentence. He aggressively answered, assuming he already knew who it was.

"What da' fuck did I say muthafucka! You think I'm playi-

"Brick!..Brick!" Yelled the female voice on the other end of the receiver.

"Baby it's me, and who in the hell got you so worked up like that?"

"Taccara," He asked dumbfoundedly as if her revelation didn't fully register.

"Yeah baby, Taccara." He paused for a second as he realized how crazy he must've sounded to her, then spoke apologetically.

"Damn, my fault baby. I slipped and let a sucka get me off my square."

49

"Who baby?" Taccara asked with concern in her voice.

"It don't even matter baby. But whassup with you"

"Just missin' you that's all baby. So can I come thru?"

"Yeah baby, fall thru so you can do what you do best and get a guy mind right."

"Okay, I'll see you in a bit."

"Fasho, holla."

"Which one was that whoadie?" Tef asked in a deep New Orleans drawl.

"That was my main one playa. The one I met at Pappadeax in Houston last year."

"Oh yeah, the one wit' da' cute smile and long tongue?"

"Yeah nigga, and the fat ass and good pussy." They both chuckled at Brick's response.

"Man, she was makin' them shrimp look so good twirlin' that long-ass tongue around'em. I had to holla at'er to get a demonstration of her headwork. And needless to say, when I finally got the demo, she took the number one spot from Tanisha silly ass." Brick grinned as he came to the final twist in the blunt he was rolling... He licked it, put a flame under it from the lighter to seal the deal, then sparked it up.

"Sup!..Sup! Oowee! This dat' good ass cushy uushy boy, doin' what it do baby." Brick squawked with calm emphasis as he began to cough from the heavy inhalation of smoke.

"These white owls burn good-n-slow just how I like it." Brick elaborated on the moment a bit more in a strained voice before casually passing the blunt to Tef, disregarding the fact that Tef don't indulge... He shrugged his shoulders and took another deep toke upon Tef's silent refusal, then blew out the remnants of smoke a few moments later as Tef took a big swallow from the bottle of apple juice he nursed as if it was liquor.

Brick cracked his side in laughter as he leaned side-ways on the leather couch and pointed at Tef's bottle of apple juice. He was attempting to speak about how much Tef enjoyed his juice, but he couldn't get the words pass his convulsing stomach and slobbering mouth. The cush had him caught up in its elements and he was right where he wanted to be as he laughed hysterically at Tef.

Thirty minutes after the blunt was gone, Taccara arrived, and Brick didn't waiste any time leading her to the bedroom.   Meanwhile, Brick's soldiers steadily ran to different cars and served everybody from fiends to other dealers. The excessive activity had the block ripe for a come up. They were running through their supply of coke so fast, that they were hoping Brick would have another connect before they ran out.

Shawn stood back in the cut and watched El and the rest of the crew handle business while he stood on patrol and made sure things went smooth... He reached up and adjusted his doo-rag over his thick braids, then lit up a Newport and let his eyes canvass the area for any unwanted or uninvited guest. A few moments later, a cocaine-white 760iL cruised by real slow with four patrons inside. Shawn instantly recognized the driver as one of Mr. Alverez's top workers. His name was Gooch, and he was completely loyal to Mr. Alverez and all that he stood for... Shawn slid back a little deeper into the furrow of the tenement building that he stood beside to slightly conceal his identity a bit more. He didn't want Gooch to notice his presence as he peered at them from the cut to see what they wanted on this side of town.

Gooch came to a slow stop where all the hustle and bussle was taking place and motioned for one of the youngsta's to come to the car... The youngsta known as Pig eagerly approached his car a few moments later.

"Whuddup Gooch. What's poppin?"

"Ain't nothin' youngsta' same shit different day, ya' dig. But peep this, I just came through to holla on that yola tip, feel me? My people outta work right now, but one of my lil dudes wanna get about eighteen o's the hard way, and he'a be through here in about a hour to holla if it's all good. So would it be a problem for yall to accommodate him?"

"Naw Gooch, just make the order and we'a make da' move. We damn near more efficient than Mickey D's baby. So tell yo' dude to fall through and we got'em, a'ight."

"A'ight youngsta good lookin.' Holla." As the beemer pulled off, one of Gooch's cronies known as Ice winked at Pig from the passenger side as his diamond-filled necklace, bracelet, watch, and earrings glistened and damn near blinded him. Ice and Gooch favored each other in appearance and would often be labeled as family-members... They were both dark-complected dudes with low fades, over six-feet in height, with nice bankrolls and hard features.

Shawn immediately stepped to El and made inquiries about their visit as soon as they left, then told El he could go get the last two-kilos from Brick, so they did.

El, Silk, and a few of Brick's other youngsta's arrived at the safe house about fifteen minutes after Taccara... Tef counted up the money they'd dropped off and told them to chill until Brick comes out of the bedroom with Taccara, so they kicked-back until further notice.

Brick watched Taccara intently as she swayed her well proportioned hips and ass seductively toward the bedroom mirror... Her French-vanilla skin, juicy lips and almond-shaped eyes complimented her short, feathered haircut well.

When she slid off her short purple leather jacket, Brick hissed at the better view of the purple thong that peeked out the top of her low-rider jeans. He walked up behind her and placed his eager hands around her small waiste and pressed his limp member against her soft plump backside. She willingly pressed herself back against him and slowly rolled her ass on him as she watched the lust grow in his eyes through the reflection in the mirror. He sucked on her neck then licked around her earlobe because he knew it was the spot to get her worked up. Taccara let out a soft moan along with a passionate-

"Ss..Oow boy you know that's my spot." Brick didn't say a word, he just continued to lick around her spot and let his roaming hands slide up her stomach to cuff her hefty breast's. He was tired of the foreplay, so he suddenly released her and took a few steps backward... The moment she turned around and faced him, he mouthed,

"Take that shit off." Then immediately began taking his own clothes off... In a matter of minutes, they both were naked. Brick layed flat on his back and watched Taccara's breast's swing freely as she climbed on top of his pole and straddled him. Brick instantly gripped her soft ass-cheeks and thrusted himself upward into her slippery hole with a stiff pump.

Taccara grunted as he thrusted again... again... again... and again. Her volumptous ass shook like jelly as Brick continued to push himself aggressively into her. Taccara's intentions was to ride him like a professional rodeo-girl, but his belligerent approach caught her off guard and wouldn't allow her to find her intended rhythm. All she could do was howl to the top of her lungs and lean forward in a lazy slumber as Brick fiercely dug into her wet, tight, inviting flesh.

Brick went on like that for twenty-minutes, then placed her in the doggy-style position and began pounding her from behind, causing her ass-cheeks to jiggle and her head to jerk forward.

"Ungh! Ungh! Ooh shit! Ooh shit! Ooh shit! ...You fuckin' me so good Brick! Keep doin' it! Keep doin' it! ... Keep ... aww! Fuck dis' pussy Brick! Fuck it! Ungh!"

Taccara gripped the bedsheets tightly as Brick fucked her from behind as if he was pissed at her about something.

"Like dat! Huh bitch? Like dat!" He asked scornfully as he roughly slammed himself into her harder... Tef and the rest of the occupants of the house sat around smokin' marijuana and listening to Fifty-Cent's *'Get Rich or Die Tryin'* CD until El suddenly got up and turned the music down and shooshed everyone, summing them to quiet down as he pointed toward the bedroom-door with a slight smirk on his face... Within moments they were all at the door listening to the wild untamed sex-session that came from the room.

"Ghaddamn whoadie, my nigga smashin' dat bitch." Tef whispered in a heavy New Orleans accent as he tuned in closer to her mixture of moans and screams.

As they listened further, each of them began unconsciously tugging at their own privates as they went into their own personal fantasies of her. Wishing it was them fuckin' the dime-piece instead of Brick and wondering if they would be able to cause her to carry on like that or not. They stayed transfixed for the next twenty-minutes until Brick finally bust his second and final nut, then they all walked away exchanging silly grins and whispering comments as they each tried to conceal their individual erections...

Brick and Taccara came out of the bedroom ten minutes afterwards.

"Fire up some smoke fools." Said Brick as he walked through the living-room with his shirt off exposing his slender tattoo'd frame, and creased abdominals.

"Somebody seems to be pretty amped-up since they got they jollies off man." Said El in a joking manner. Taccara wore a bothered expression on her face as Brick and his cronies' cracked jokes and smoked more cush... A few moments later, Taccara stood up and walked beside the bedroom door they'd previously emerged from.

"Brick." She calmly called out as Brick and his partners all rocked and bobbed their heads to a song by *Jadakiss featuring Beanie Siegal...* Brick heard her, but he was all wrapped up in the song so he ignored her.

"Brick!" She shouted this time, causing him to respond in a snappy tone.

"What girl."

"Comeer for a minute, I need to talk to you."

"Damn baby, don't you see I'm 'bout to handle some business with my dawgs." Brick spoke up irritably again because he felt that he knew what her issue was, and really wasn't up for it.

"Well you can get right back to yo' business after I holla atchu, it's only gon' take a minute."

"Damn Taccara!" shouted Brick as he went to see what she wanted...

The moment Taccara closed the bedroom door, El turned towards Tef with red eyes and a silly grin and squawked,

"Damn dawg, that bitch must got a white-liver or somethin,' she can't get enough of the big homie." They all released low chuckles after El's comment, then immediately turned the music back down and darted back over to the bedroom door.

"Come on Taccara don't start that shit again."

"Naw fuck dat shit Brick. I told you before I don't like to be called no bitch, period!"

Girl you know that ain't nothin' but a figure-of-speech for me when I say that shit to you. I was caught-up in the moment baby, and it just seem like dat pussy get wetter when I call you a bitch while I'm bussin' dat thang up. So stop trippin' 'bout dat' petty shit, you know it ain't shit."

"Well for yo' information Brick, my pussy don't get no wetter when you say that word to me. If anything, my shit gets dry. So for the fifty-eth fuckin' time, don't call me nomore bitches, alright!" Brick huffed heavily before responding.

"I really don't see why you trippin,' especially wit' all that freaky-shit you be sayin' while we fuckin,' *'Oh fuck me Brick! Fuck this pussy hard baby. Oh Brick I like the way you fuckin me!'* Brick mocked her in a whiny voice while makin' his point.

"Whateva' Brick, but can you please just respect what I said. That's all I ask of you."

Brick didn't respond, he just attempted to walk out the door, but she swiftly jumped in front of him, blocking his path.

"So what's it gon' be Brick? Huh?" ...Now clearly heated, Brick slowly focused on her intently, wearing a blank expression on his agitated face. He stared into her eyes for 30 seconds without saying a word... Then without warning, he suddenly snatched her clothes off in a belligerent manner and wrestled her into the doggy-style position on the bed again.

After a few moments of struggling, Taccara screamed to the top of her lungs as she felt his hard flesh tear forcibly into her unlubricated asshole.

"Bitch!...slam! Bitch!...slam! Bitch!...slam! Bitch!!" Brick gripped her waist tightly and savagely slammed himself into her tight anus without mercy. He yelled out-

"Bitch!" with every thrust he delivered, and the fresh blood that leaked from her ass seemed to make him push harder.

El and other crew members all fell to the floor in hysterical laughter as they listened to their commander-in-chief put down the brutal demonstration on Taccara. They quietly cheered him on as her horrific screams continued to echo pass the door throughout the contours of the house.

The beastly assault went on nonstop for about fifteen-minutes before it finally came to an end. Then Brick made his way up to her face, breathing heavily as he casually lifted her chin, listening to her sniffle in a low, steady cry.

"Now you listen the fuck up, and you listen good...Bitch!. If it was a square that you was lookin' to fall in love with, you shoulda' went to church and found you one. And if you was misunderstood as to who or what I was when you started fuckin' wit' me, let me put you the fuck up on game. When you fell in love with me, you fell in love with a muthafuckin' street-nigga, flat-out. Now go clean yo'self up and act the fuck like you know before I put another demo down on yo' sensitive ass. And don't ever again in yo' corny-ass life tell me what da' fuck to say outta my mouth."

Brick paused for a moment before exiting the room because he assumed his cronies were at the door listening, and he wanted to give them ample time to scamper back to their seats without getting caught by him. He actually wanted them to hear what took place in the bedroom, because the way he handled it only added more validity and credibility to his underworld leadership-position.

He really liked Taccara because he knew she was over-all a genuine, good woman. But he knew he couldn't afford to let his soldiers see the slightest amount of sorrow in him no matter what. Especially during times when a major war was brewing for them. Anything along the lines of *love, compassion, desire,* or *unbridled affection* towards a woman would eventually be misconstrued and labeled as *weakness* on his part... Which in his mind, would cause his soldiers to start *undermining* his decisions, and question his leadership ability altogether. Then shortly afterwards, the respect that they once had for him would diminish.

And *history has shown us repeatedly, that no leader can remain a leader without the loyalty and respect of his soldiers...*

When Brick came out the room, he casually walked up to El, and retrieved the less-than-half of lit blunt from him.

After taking a few drags and analyzing each of their faces, he received a feeling of satisfaction because their demeanors told him they had no doubts about the strength of their leader.

"Yo' Duke," He called out.

"Whuddup big homie." Answered Duke.

"You say yall got a sale for eighteen the hard way, right."

"Yeah big homie, that's a fact."

"A'ight then, let's get at dat paper dawg. Tef, meet us in the kitchen A.S.A.P, 'da grind don't stop."

They all showed up in the kitchen ten minutes later and rolled up more marijuana while Tef put the necessary tools in place to begin his work.

Brick got excited as always whenever he'd watch his lil crony work his magic in the kitchen. Tef constantly broke-off chunks of the potent cocaine and dropped it into the large pyrex pot. He kept a blank expression as he watched the water began to boil to a higher degree through the clear Pyrex glass...

A few moments later, the cocaine slowly sunk to the bottom of the pan and turned into a gel-form as it all began to merge together. Brick took another pull off the blunt and replied,

"Don't take ya' eyes off that lil nigga man, just watch his work, he'a beast at that shit." Brick steadily focused on Tef excitedly as he began adding more measured amounts of baking soda and another white powder-substance, while simultaneously stirring the contents with an eggbeater. He made whipping circular motions as he stood over the pot in full concentration mode. He whipped, whipped, and whipped until he was fully satisfied with the results of the product. Then he began adding ice-cubes to cool down the temperature of the water... He continued to stir slowly, all while adding the ice cubes.

As the stretched nine ounces began to harden, Tef stopped stirring and placed the pan under the water faucet and let cold water run over the product. A few moments later, what started out as nine-ounces of cocaine was now eighteen ounces of cocaine... Brick leaped up from the chair he was sitting in upon completion of the cook-out, ecstatic.

"I told yall boy! My lil nigga don't be bullshitten! Chef Boy-R-Tef nigga! Yall niggas betta recognize." After the product was fairly dry, El separated it, bagged it up and hurried back to the block with the others to make the sale...

While they waited for Gooch's people to show up, Pig, Silk, Moe, Pep, and Shoe controlled the heavy traffic and made individual sales while Shawn stood in the cut and watched their backs...

Shawn casually pulled out his cellphone and answered it... It was Brick.

"Whuddup Shawn, what it look like on yo' end?"

"It's all good Brick, we gon' need dat' last thang-and-a-half shortly cause it's out here doin' what it do dawg."

"Bet dat up dawg, just send one of the youngsta's to come get it whenever, it'a be here, aight."

"A'ight fasho. But check this out big dawg, by no means am I tryna' question yo' judgement, but do you really trust conversating on your phone on the work tip like that?"

"Under normal circumstances, naw. But under fixed circumstances, yeah."

"Whatchu mean by fixed, Brick?"

"What I mean is, I paid a lot of money for a lil device I got installed in my phone that will over-ride any extra listening-parties and distort shit. It's something like shooting a virus in your phone. It basically scrambles shit and makes everything you say sound like gibberish. It was designed by them Brittish muhfuckas, they'a beast wit' shit like that. So like I said young dawg, it's all good over here... Anyway, did El nem' move them eighteen yet?"

"Naw, not yet they still waitin' on Gooch people to fall through and get it."

Brick suddenly positioned himself upright in the chair he was in and pressed the phone firmly against his ear and asked,

"Whatchu mean waitin' on Gooch people to come get it... Is we talkin' 'bout the same Gooch... Black-ass Gooch who down wit' Mr. Alverez?"

"Yeah, that Gooch." Answered Shawn skeptically.

"Dawg, that nigga Gooch ain't never mediated no punk-ass 18-ounce deal, that's beneath his standards. Somethin' ain't right about that one. Yall niggas fall ba—Tat! Tat! Tat! Tat! Tat! Tat! Boh! Boh! Boh! ...

"Oh shit!" was all Brick heard from Shawn, along with the rapid gunfire before the phone went dead seconds later... Brick jumped up and attempted to go inform Tef on what had just took place when suddenly, Brrrr!... Brrrr! Boh! Boh! Boh! Boh! Boh! Brick hit the floor as the flurry of gunfire shattered windows and cut through the house like shears through flesh. He instantly crawled and shielded his face from the shattered pieces of flying glass as he attempted to make it to his SKS...

Bullets flew in from the Northeast corner of the house, as well as the Northwest corner of the house, which indicated to him that it was more than one shooter, and they were within close proximity to the house. Making it extremely difficult for him to maneuver freely...

The shooting suddenly ceased for a moment, and Brick felt that it would be a good opportunity to make it to the bedroom to get his weapon, so he suddenly came up out of his crawling position and ran in a low crouch as fast as he could to the bedroom. But just as he got there, the gunfire viciously peppered the house again, causing him to instantly drop flat on the floor and cover his head from the flurry of bullets...

One of the gunmen suddenly stuck his fully automatic mac-11 through the bedroom window and made a sweeping gesture across the room. All Brick could do was ball-up and wait for the pressure to let up again...

A few seconds later, the fierce gunfire paused again. And Brick didn't hesitate to resume crawling again, only this time very slow because his intuition told him it was a bluff to make any survivors in the house move prematurely, to get caught by another unexpected flurry of slugs... And surely enough, he was right. The weapons blasted off again, and Brick clawed and scathed the floor as he steadily inched his way toward the head of the bed where the SKS nestled slothly against the wall... He suddenly felt something wet and thick in his path... then he felt a lump of flesh that appeared to be soaked in a fluid that he was all too familiar with. He peeked his head up during the chaotic attack, and his heart skipped a beat when he saw Taccara's beautiful specimen of a body soaked in blood.

Her eyes were open as she laid there lifeless, and Brick silently concluded that the massive hole near her temple is what more-than-likely sealed her fate.

As he gathered himself and attempted to inch his way around her, another flurry of bullets suddenly came directly at him, riddling Taccara's already deceased corpse again and rocking her violently instead of hitting him.

Brick cringed at the sight but didn't have time to allow his emotions to cloud his thinking. He just stayed low and continued to snake his way toward his weapon... His efforts were nothing short of laborious, yet in vain because by the time he made it to his weapon, he didn't even get a chance to return fire because the shooters were long gone.

In the aftermath of the incident, he was thankful that Tef was alright. But losing Taccara in that fashion really had him distraught and empathetic over her. And on top of her calamity, he lost his whole crew in the fierce attack on the block simultaneously. The only survivors were him, Shawn, and Tef. His mind was boggled, and he needed to take refuge fast... So he immediately placed Tef and Shawn in another safe house, then informed them that he'd be back in a couple days. He had to regroup and clear his head so he could fully envision his countermove on Mr. Alverez. And he knew in his heart that whatever it was he'd come with, it would not only have to make some serious noise... But would have to be exaltingly, and solemnly loud.

Chapter 6

"SS, mmh... ooh Ray Ray, yeah baby.. yes... SSS...
Ungh!" Sheila squawked and moaned as Ray Ray
kept her legs pinned back while he thrusted himself
deeper and deeper into the contours of her wet flesh.
Her soft body rocked and her hefty breast's shook
violently with every aggressive thrust he delivered.

Sheila was skillful with her sexual prowess, and Ray
Ray drove into her deeply as her pleasure-box gave
him all that he anticipated... She stayed in sequence
with his backward motion, and the pleasurable
sensation it gave his member always got him more
excited with every passing second... Sheila would
normally wait until they were at least 45 minutes into
the session before she would begin working the
magic between her beautiful brown double-jointed
legs. But her raging hormones caused her to go for it
early tonight...

They lost control momentarily, then found a compatible rhythm and pumped each other savagely through a series of grunts and moans, lustfully in each other's ear. They went on for an hour straight as fresh sweat dripped from their bodies, and freely spilled into the green prada sheets as if their bodies were melting.

Her quavering voice in his ear told him she was fast approaching her third orgasm, and he wasn't far behind.

"Oow! Get ... this... pussy... Ray Ray! You.. uh! You.. Know... How... I, ah! Like it! You know baby! ...You know how... ooooooooooh!" Sheila's body jerked violently as the powerful orgasm exploded from her hole and covered Ray Ray's hard flesh with her sweet nectar... And only a few seconds afterwards, Ray Ray's body obediently followed suit.

Sheila immediately pulled his member from her sex and aimed it at her stomach and breast's. She aided his release as she pumped his pipe with her hand, causing the thick, milky semen to burst forward from his tool and successfully spray her tities and stomach the way she liked it.

As Ray Ray remained in a push-up position, elevated above her heaving body. Sheila rubbed his nut all over her breast and stomach as she smiled at him devilishly and watched the sweat glisten off his chiseled pecs... They showered together afterwards, then curled up next to each other as the evening sky made an inevitable transition into a murky firmament.

Sheila laid wide awake in deep thought as Ray Ray released a light snore and slept peacefully next to her. She could not seem to fall asleep and constantly brushed against Ray Ray in a brusque manner as she tossed and turned in search of comfort. The sound of Ray Ray's unexpected groggy voice slightly startled her as he mumbled to her in the darkness.

"What's wrong bae?" ...Sheila suddenly ceased all movement and remained quiet without giving a response. She wasn't sure if he was awake or just talking in his sleep, until he spoke up again.

"I know you up Sheila. And I know you got somethin' on ya' mind cause you keep poking me in my side with them pointy-ass elbows. Now whassup, tell me what's wrong."

Sheila smiled and released a light chuckle as she admired her man's humor and accurate familiarity with her ways. She slowly scooted closer to him and wrapped herself around the warmth of his relaxed frame.

"Okay baby. You've exposed me and I'm ready to vent." She cleared her throat as Ray Ray remained silent, waiting to hear her issue.

"Baby I've been dreamin' about my parents lately. And in most of the dreams, my mother seems so sad. I truly don't know what to make of it. What do you think baby?"

"I think you just missin' your parents and you wanna' see'em. And I think this is your indirect way of asking me can you see'em." Sheila made an embarrassed face in the darkness as Ray Ray's on-target-truth further exposed her intentions.

"Am I right Sheila?"

"Yee-es Ray Ray, I guess so." She answered in a hesitant manner.

"Well check this out Sheila, the last time that we discussed this, what conclusion did we come up with?" Sheila paused momentarily, then answered in a slow, unexcited tone.

"We came up with, it would be a bad idea because we are both fugitives. And more-than-likely the feds are still doing random sweeps of their area. And it's always better to be safe than sorry, right?"

"Right, so why you even bring it up?"

Sheila didn't answer, she just casually slid over to the other side of the bed and turned over facing the opposite direction. She curled-up in the fetal position and held her pillow tight as quiet tears cascaded down her beautiful brown face...

Ray Ray knew she was highly upset, but he made no attempt to console her. He figured he'd let her be, and maybe she'd see the logic in his reasoning in the morning.

*****

Two days later. 3pm

A constant flow of tears ran down the faces of Sheila and her mother as they held each other tightly in an overjoyed embrace. Sheila's father stood by in an emotion-filled state and watched the two most remarkable women in his life intently without saying a word.

Sheila's parents were the mild-mannered type in their elderly years. And would always opt to make things as less-complicated as possible. Her father was an ex-military person, who was known for his heroic efforts during his time in service. His colleagues nicknamed him Midnight-express because of his dark complexion and effective late-night assaults on the enemy in the gulf war. His government name is Hank Cooper... He met Sheila's mother Martha shortly after he was honorably discharged from the military. She was a registered nurse and looked identical to the way Sheila looked today.

Hank was enthralled by her beauty and subtle character and stayed persistent in his pursuit of her heart until she completely surrendered. Hank and Martha were old fashion and they felt that as long as a man and woman was age-appropriate when they found their soulmate, they should always follow their heart. So they fully understood the sparkle that gleamed from their only daughters' eyes whenever she saw or even spoke about Ray Ray in his absence. And they never once contested her choice in her mate.

After fifteen minutes of an over-emotional reunion, Sheila introduced her children to their grandparents for the very first time. They all expressed love and joy for one another as the long overdue reunion transpired. Then after catching up on things and getting emotions in check, they all had a dinner that consisted of grilled salmon, brown fried rice, garlic butter-rolls, and a Meditteranian salad... Ray Ray truly understood where Sheila learned her cooking-skills from. Her mother was a beast in the kitchen, and it was nothing less than a treat to experience her work.

After washing the meal down with a smooth red wine and grape minute-maid for the children, they all discussed how dangerous it would be to stay too long due to their fugitive status, so they prepared to leave with the promise of returning another day... Ray Ray casually excused himself and stepped in the bathroom. A few moments later, a knock at the door caused everyone to momentarily look toward the door with confused expressions... All except Hank because even though it had been a few months since his last visit, he'd recognized his nephew's distinct knock. So once he confirmed who it was with a simple

"Who is it?" he opened the door and let him in.

"Hey unc, what's goin' on witcha?" He asked after a brief hug was exchanged between them.

"Ah, same ol' same ol' nephew. How 'bout you?" You still chasin' the American dream?"

"As always unc, it's the only thing that's close to logic in my life. Other than that, it's all good." He chose not to discuss his street problems with his uncle.

Hank smiled and gave a slight nod before responding.

"Anyhow, it's good to see you nephew. And I'm glad you came through 'cause look who's here." He gestured towards Sheila, and Brick's eyes lit up when he saw his cousin that he hadn't seen since they were small children. He ran over to her excitedly and mouthed.

"Sheila, is that you couz!"

"Sheila looked at him and immediately knew who he was from his distinct birthmark.

"Brick!" She squawked excitedly. Then embraced him tightly with an overwhelming sense of compassion for her favorite cousin. They smiled at one another giddily as they looked each other over in an attempt to figure out where to begin.

"Daayumm couz" said Brick as he continued to stare and admire how beautiful of a woman she'd grown into.

"Wow, you lookin' luvely as ever couz. And I see right now I'ma have some problems out here, keepin' these lames up off you, fo'real." Sheila smiled sincerely at his compliments before responding.

"That's whassup couz, but you know I'm a Cooper too. So I got everything under control when it comes to these lames. Oh, and besides that, my husband ain't no slouch either. So I'm a Cooper slash Thompson, a force to be reckoned with couz. And speakin' of my king, I want you to meet him."

Ray Ray had just exited the bathroom and calmly approached them... Sheila introduced them respectfully with a bright smile, and the moment they shook hands, they both paused for a moment. Ray Ray immediately recognized him, and Brick immediately recognized Ray Ray's eyes...

He briefly flashed back to the day the gunman single-handedly neutralized the police and stole the large sum of Mr. Alverez's money. Which was the very reason he was goin' through all of the bullshit that he was currently goin' through. He tried not to let his suddenly changed expression give away what his mind had just recollected, so he cleared his throat and pulled out his phone as if he was checking a text message or something. Then asked to be excused for a sec as he stepped in the living-room.

"His mind was in overdrive now, and he was trippin' hard about how small the world could truly be at times... His heart raced and his adrenaline surged as he swiftly searched his thoughts to find a logical solution to his complexed predicament. He mumbled under his breath about the fact that it was truly him, *and he could actually get his ass right now.*

"*This muthafucka.*" He continued to ramble to himself.

"*Damn... How am I gon' handle this shit?*" He stayed in deep thought for another two full minutes before coming to a silent conclusion.

"*Fuck it. Sheila just gonna have to understand when I slump this nigga, cause I can't let this muhfucka get away... It's now or never, fuck it.*" Brick carefully retrieved the sixteen-shot 40 caliber from his waiste without being noticed... He took a deep breath, then slowly turned in their direction to make his move... But before he could fully complete the turn, he suddenly felt the barrel of Ray Ray's ten shot 45 pressed aggressively against his ribcage. Then felt the warmness of his breath on his ear as he whispered in a low tone.

"Not so fast homeboy, cause that silly shit that you thinkin' right now gon' get you slumped nigga. Now, I want you to slowly, and I mean slowly muthafucka... Hand me that heater, butt-first nigga."

Brick was not only shocked, he was pissed at himself for letting Ray Ray get the ups on him for a second time. He squoze his teeth together and cursed silently under his breath as the reality of the situation weighed in on him.

He knew that he was fighting a losing battle and that it would be foolish to make any false moves. So he breathed a heavy unenthused sigh of defeat, then slowly handed over his weapon to Ray Ray.

"Good choice." Said Ray Ray sarcastically. Then inconspicuously directed Brick to transition back to the living room to further their discussion.

"A'ight, check this out homie, I'ma make a long story short, and put you up on how I got to this point. And we can do one of two things after this. We can come up with a solution that would be beneficial for both of us, or I can say fuck it and rock yo' noodles right here, right now, it's on you playa... Now listen up."

--After Ray Ray explained everything to Brick, Brick actually had a new-found level of respect for him. He even found himself in a cordial state of admiration for Ray Ray and felt that two real soldiers like themselves could not only give Mr. Alverez a run for his money, but they could get the streets locked down on a level that hadn't been done in a very long time. Ray Ray even explained to Brick how he was able to rob the cops so effectively for Mr. Alverez's money. It was because those cops were working for Mr. Alverez, otherwise they would've had an army of back-up on the scene, Ray Ray detailed... Brick was flabbergasted when he found out that Mr. Alverez had actually set him up. Ray Ray and Brick concluded their conversation by agreeing to build a solid crew in order to be effective in their efforts. So they shook hands to solidify the new understanding between them, then focused on going forward with bringing the mission into fruition.

When Sheila emerged from the bathroom, she was pleased to see her man and her cousin getting along. Although she was none-the-wiser of how close things had come to poppin' off right there in her parents' house.

Loyalty Ain't Loyal Enough

Sheila smiled to herself and felt good about being around genuine family... Brick stayed for about thirty-minutes longer, then left to meet-up with a few stand-up guys that he felt would be good for the new crew.

Chapter 7

Although Ray Ray didn't like clubs, he still agreed to meet-up with Brick at a club in downtown Detroit called club Envy. Because he was aware of the benefits the loud atmosphere provided if a person wanted their conversations muffled in case of wiretaps. And that's just what he wanted, so he rolled with it.

After a short frisk from the bouncers, Ray Ray made his way to the VIP section of the club where Brick and two of the potential new members were sitting with two of his current members.

"Whuddup doe my guy." Said Brick as he stood-up and slapped five with Ray Ray. He casually turned toward the crew and began introducing everybody by name.

Okay homie, this dude right here is my young gun, the real Teflon Don. We call him Tef... This my other fasho rida, we call him Shawn... This my nigg Chop.

And this my dawg Adolph. I did time wit' both of these dudes up in Kinross State Prison on a punk-ass pistol case. These dudes is solid as they come... And fellas, this my guy Ray Ray. His reputation speaks for itself. And if we can all agree on getting money together, I gotta' say I fully trust his judgement on being the driver of this car. And I expect nothing less than the same from yall. We have a direction that we tryna go in. And as long as we all stay on the same page, we can take this shit to another level. So for now, let's get acquainted and start connecting the dots to a successful future together."

Adolph sucked his teeth before speaking up.

"Pst, pst... So when you say, 'bein' the driver of the car homie,' You basically sayin' dawg gon' be our boss huh?" Brick silently thought to himself,

"Here go this Beanie Sigel lookin' ass nigga." before he slowly turned to him and said,

"Yeah homie, somethin' like that." Adolph twirled the toothpick around in his mouth and smirked before responding.

"Well turn some muthafuckin' drinks up dude and let me see if this nigga really *'boss worthy.'*... ha ha ha." Adolph was wild as fuck and literally had no conscience. He would often-times say many offensive things out of his mouth before ever giving it any thought... But Brick was used to his behavior and never took it personal. But to the people who didn't know him, they read him as distastefully rude, and wouldn't particularly care for his company.

Ray Ray smirked at Adolph's comment, then glanced around at the atmosphere and reflected back to the last time him and Smoke was in a club together... *He thought about how Smoke got apprehended by the authorities that night and ended up doing five years on a seven-year bid in state prison. Ray Ray hated the fact that Smoke was now deceased, and he knew in his heart that he would never stop hunting the man responsible. In fact, he thought about the upcoming meeting he had in two weeks with one of Smoke's most trusted friends. A man from Argentina named Teko.*

Teko went to great lengths to contact Ray Ray after Smoke's death. And even though he was a major drug-dealer, Ray Ray still accepted an invite to have a discussion with him. Because he knew that Teko could possibly be the key to getting to Mr. Alverez... Teko wanted to meet with Ray Ray because he explained that he had a proposition for him. But of course, he declined to discuss anything on the phone. So Ray Ray would find out the order-of-business when the meeting took place.

As they sat there in the VIP section of the club, Brick smiled when he noticed the tall, slim, browncomplected dude with a low fade come in his direction. It was a dude named Chuck that he met through some of his relatives in the Mack-n-Mitchell area. Dude use to be a thorough money-gettin' guy. And Brick silently hoped he was still on the same shit.

"Whuddup doe my dawg." Said Chuck as he slapped five with Brick and gave a short G-embrace.

"Ain't shit my guy, still tryna' get it, you know me. And hopefully yo' resume' didn't change Chuck. Cause I'm tryna' grab something from you ASAP if you still gettin' down."

"Man, that's all I know." Said Chuck as he smiled and moved closer to Brick's ear.

"Whatchu tryna' grab?"

"Well, for starters, a half-a-brick of that white-girl. And once I know it's A-1, I'm in a position to grab at least ten from you if you can handle a order that size."

Chuck gave off an expression that suggested he could handle any size order. Then abruptly started callin' out his cellphone number and promised to hit him up in a few days.

Ray Ray and Brick concluded their business that night and also made plans to meet-up again in one week at one of the new safe-houses that Brick purchased.

Two days later...

After Brick ended the call with Chuck, he explained to Tef that Chuck was gonna' meet him in the parking lot of McDonald's off I-75 and Mack, to do the transaction. Brick told Tef not to even go through all of the quality-check precautions that they would normally go through because he was in a hurry to get the deal done. So he was basically goin' off blind faith this time... Tef agreed, then left...

Tef was already in the drop area, so he made it to the destination in ten minutes and 31 seconds. —After he pulled in a parking spot and shifted the car in park, Chuck casually emerged from the doors of McDonald's eating on a quarter-pounder, with a Mc'Donald's bag in hand. He walked to the passenger-side of the black charger Tef was driving. He leaned in the window, pulled the half out, laid it on the seat, then said,

"Put the money in the bag." Tef placed the thirteen thousand in the bag. And just like that, the deal was done. Everything had gone smooth as planned. At least up until Tef got the 5 percent cocaine, 80 percent sheetrock, and 15 percent flour, back to Brick...

The petty move had Brick furious. And the timing could not have been worse for *"This hoe-shit!"* is what Brick hissed as he dialed Chuck's number for the 8th time without an answer.

"Dawg, I want all eyes lookin' fa' dat bitch-nigga 24-7 'til yall find him. Damn!!"

Brick slammed his balled-up fist down on the table as he looked in the opposite direction of his new crew. Then took a couple gulps of the fifth of Hennessey to wash down the two percasets that he'd just tossed in his mouth.

Adolph twirled the toothpick around in his mouth with a slight smirk as he mouthed.

"I told you to let me handle that move dawg. But it's all good, he got dat off on the young dawg. But we'a find dat pussy. In the meantime, just hurry up and get some coke on the floe, a nigga tryna eat." A few lingering seconds of silence passed by without either one of them sayin' a word. Then Adolph suddenly blurted out,

"Let me ask you somethin' Brick. How is this nigga Ray Ray gon' be a boss over anything we got goin' on if he ain't about slangin' no yae?"

Brick knew that it was a logical question, and he already had an answer for Adolph because he knew where his mind was at.

"Dawg, it really ain't a boss thang. It's just that I respect his knowledge in some of the most critical elements of the game. So just roll with the flow for now Adolph. Cause quiet-as-kept, if everything go as planned, you can build your own crew in about six months from now, facts nigga." Adolph nodded in agreement, then took a deep inhale off the blunt he was smoking... He spoke-up again after exhaling the smoke.

"Okay my dawg, that sounds just peachy, but peep this. Whenever we do get back on, I got a bitch that's the truth when it comes to cooking-up the work. You should really consider usin' her." Brick took a sip from the glass of Hen before responding.

"No thanks my dawg. My lil nigga Tef is all I need on that tip. He'a beast wit' dat shit, real talk." Adolph rubbed his head in an agitated fashion, then calmly said,

"Well let me know if you change yo' mind dawg. Cause the bitch I'm talkin' 'bout a beast too."

"Fasho my dawg."

---As Ray Ray sat and reflected on the recent events, he'd read Adolph like a book. And he knew that the ambitions of certain men could sometimes compromise a good organization. And he was well aware that in this business, it was a bonus if you could actually like a business associate. But it definitely wasn't a necessity.

Chapter 8

Adolph and Chop pulled up in the midst of muscle cars at the Saturday night street-races on Mt. Elliot near the I-94 freeway. They were in a silver GTO Mustang with a hyped-up engine and modified performance parts. It was more tweeked than today's V8, 700 horsepower, six-speed transmission hellcat.

There were a bunch of street hustlers on the scene with tricked-out exotic cars. And they were eager to demonstrate what was under their hoods... Engines roared, music blarred, and marijuana smoke permeated the air.

Sexy females with curvy bodies strolled around hoping to get tips for callin' a race. And were looking just as pretty as the cars that were racing...

As Adolph and Chop conversated with a few different dudes, a dude from the St. Jean and Warren area name Dee-Dee pulled up beside Adolph in a rose-red ZR-1 corvette and spoke-up.

"Whuddup doe Adolph, you feelin' lucky tonight?"

Adolph smirked at his comment as he twirled the toothpick in his mouth before responding.

"Shid my nigga, the question is, how lucky you feelin' tonight. Cause I don't believe in luck, I believe in Adolph."

"Ha Ha, that's the spirit my dawg. So, what you wanna' put up on a go?"

"Nigga what the fuck you think, titles nigga. You know I'm a all-or-nothin' kinda' nigga." Dee-Dee paused for a second, then smiled and said,

"Okay playa, let's get it poppin." Adolph pointed at a female that was a Megan Good look-alike and gestured for her to call the race.

After they lined the cars up side by side, she strolled over to them wearing six-inch *B-Tarvino* stilleto heels, low-rider blue-jeans, and a short leather holter-top... She walked up between both of the vehicles, then addressed both drivers.

"Okay fellas, yall know the drill. Only pull off on my command. No car-to-car contact. And in the name and spirit of dignity, both drivers return to the starting point of the race... Understood?"

They both nodded in agreement, then the sexy woman slowly walked backwards until she was at the front of both cars. Adolph was on the right, and Dee-Dee was on the left. The engines roared ferociously from both cars, as the sexy woman held up her hands as a precursor to the start of the race.

Both men had their game-face's on, and Adolph twirled the toothpick in his mouth with eager-anticipation... *Brrmmm! Brrmmm!* ...The cars were ready, and the drivers were more ready. *Brrmmm! Brrrmmm! Brrrmm! Brrrmm!---Skrrrrrrrrrrrrrrr!!*

Both cars leaped forward as the well-manicured hands dropped to the woman's side... Dee-Dee was slightly ahead as they both accelerated through the thick clouds of white smoke. Getting up to speeds of over a hundred miles an hour in less than 6 seconds.

Adolph just smiled and twirled his toothpick as he zoomed forward and shot pass Dee-Dee right before they crossed the designated finish-line.

"Damn!" grimaced Dee-Dee when he realized he'd lost the race... Then without giving it a second thought, he bust a wild u-turn and sped down the service-ramp on I-94, headed east.

Adolph didn't waiste any time jumping right on his trail in pursuit of the corvette... And as they raced up the freeway, maneuvering around car after car, Adolph reached down in the space between the gearbox and the seat. And came up with a sig 10-shot 45.

He quickly made a mental note that he would start firing at Dee-Dee the moment an opportunity presented itself. They both continued to drive recklessly through traffic, and just when Adolph thought he might've saw an opportunity to fire the sig and hit his target, a lady driving a blue dodge-caravan made a lane-change without ever noticing the speeding vehicle's that were approaching fast...

Dee-Dee was able to get pass her, but Adolph found his vehicle skidding to a grinding hault to avoid an ugly accident with the van.

"Bitch!" He cursed out loud as he aggressively wrestled the car back under control. And bein' that he was momentarily held up, he was now at least seven cars behind the vette...

By the time he began gaining traction again, he slowed back down when he noticed the Michigan State Trooper car pulling Dee-Dee over. He glanced over at Dee-Dee as he rode pass them, then mumbled,

"I'll see you again bitch." Then headed back to the races to pick-up Chop.

DPD officer Smitty Branch was already on the freeway in route to a fellow officer's house when he noticed the State Troopers conducting the traffic stop.

He slowly pulled up behind them as they were allowing Dee-Dee to pull off. Smitty walked up to the trooper's vehicle and smiled when he noticed the Ukranian trooper named Ducinski, and his Asian partner named Dressner.

"What's up fellas." Smitty spoke as he leaned in toward them and rested his hands on top of their squad-car.

"I ain't never known yall to let a muthafucka pull off that quick, is everything good?" Smitty questioned the abnormalcy.

Trooper Ducinski spoke up.

"Yeah bud, everthing is fine. That dude was one of our bitches. We keep secrets together."

Smitty smirked before responding.

"Oh yeah, what kind of secrets?" Ducinski and Dressner looked at each other sarcastically before Ducinski spoke up.

"Well, let's just say that we found ourselves in the middle of an intense internal-affairs investigation not long ago because we beat the fuck out of a guy. We tased his ass about four-times, then snapped some photos of his little dick for souveneir-purposes... Needless to say, the muthafucker made a complaint about it, and not only stood to make millions from it, we almost got fired from the shit. But our bitch Dee-Dee wouldn't vouch for his side of the story, which was the only thing that saved our asses. So whenever we bump into him, if he's doing wrong we cut him a break."

Officer Smitty gave a heavy head-nod of understanding because he'd been under too many internal affairs investigations to count.

"Alright guys, I'll see yall at the bar this weekend." Said Smitty as he prepared to leave.

"Welcome back to the force bro." said Dressner before Smitty walked away... A few moments later, Dressner and Ducinski stared at each other passionately as Smitty's patrol car accelerated pass them.

"That's one ugly muthafucker." Said Ducinski as he slowly pushed Dressner's head down toward his erect member.

"Faggot muthafucka's." Mumbled Smitty as they faded in his rearview mirror.

After five minutes of Dressner sucking his partner off, a sudden thought of his FBI agent wife, caused him to lean up and say,

"You know I can't be long, I gotta' meet-up with my wife in an hour."

"Yeah Yeah, I'm almost there. Now put it back in your mouth and stop talkin' bitch before I report you to your commander for neglect of duty. They both laughed briefly, then Dressner did as he was told and continued to pleasure his partner until he flooded his corrupt mouth, with a heavy load of corrupt semen.

Moments later, they pulled off on the busy freeway and casually blended into traffic.

Chapter 9

As the dark-skinned, middle-aged attractive woman known as crack-head Anne continued to bob her head up and down on Adolph's dick, he pulled on the blunt he was smoking and groaned,

"Yeah bitch, that's whussup. Work dat hot mouth bitch. And you betta' swallow it all when I buss." The woman was skillful at what she did, and it wasn't long before Adolph's eyes was rolling in the back of his head as she swallowed every drop of his semen, then licked him clean.

Afterwards, he met up with her in the kitchen and gave her the ounce of cocaine he'd got from a stripper-chick who stole it from a caucasion trick she was with a few nights prior...

Anne grabbed the baking soda, benzo-caine, B-12, and the stainless-steel cookware and began to perform her magic... When she was done, she'd whipped the ounce of coke into four ounces, and

Adolph loved it. He told himself that whenever Brick finally got some coke on the floor, Anne would be the perfect chef to allow him to skim a significant amount of the work off the top without Brick ever knowing. He smirked to himself as he entertained the thought, then gave her a three-and-a-half gram eightball for the job.

He left and made it over to the stripper Valerie's house twenty minutes later.

"Where yo' brother at Val?" He asked as he slapped Val on her phat ass.

"He in his bedroom fuckin' wit' them damn video games-n-shit... But check this out. Whussup wit' dat work I gave you from that trick?"

"I gotchu bitch, damn. As soon as lil bro flip the shit, so chill-out broad." She gave off a subtle look before responding.

"Okay nigga, that's whussup. But on another note, when you told me to be on the look-out for anybody with some coke, I was. And my homegirl say her dude Polo straight on that tip, so you might wanna' holla at him."

Adolph formed a scolded expression before mouthing,

"You talkin' 'bout lil frail-ass Polo off the eastside who use to fuck around in Flint sometimes?"

96

"Yeah, that Polo." She answered skeptically because she never met anybody who liked him except her girl.

"Nah, I'm cool on that bitch-made nigga."

"Yeah, I know he ain't shit, but he's the only one that came across the radar. My girl told me he used to send lil niggas OT to sit in spots and wouldn't even pay them." Val attempted to validate why Adolph probably didn't like him.

"Well, I don't give a fuck about none of that. I just don't like the nigga, 'cause like I said, dude bitch-made... But if push comes to shove, and don't nothin' surface soon, put me in dat nigga's space. I'll be more-than-happy to rob dat bitch."

Val would pull off small capers from time to time, but she wasn't into setting dudes up. That was out of her league, so she just laughed his comment off, and knew that she would never bring Polo's name up again.

Adolph walked in her brother Eric's room a few moments later.

"Whuddup doe my guy, put yo' shit on and get ready to shoot a move with me. I gotta' go grab another digital scale, plus I wanna' holla atchu about something." ---They left out the house together ten minutes later.

Chapter 10

Brick met-up with Adolph, Chop, and Tef when he got the word that Gooch and a few of his homies would be attending a well-known strip-club on the Westside of Detroit...

They all sat in an idle'd vehicle with high-powered weapons, waiting for Gooch and his homies to come out... Ten minutes later, Gooch and three of his homies hopped in a black S600 benz after tipping the valet-driver, then pulled off...

Brick followed the benz for about eight blocks, then suddenly accelerated pass them in the dark gray charger, cutting them off, forcing them to hit a curve in the benz, causing it to become situated crookedly in the street...

Brick and his team emerged from the vehicle swiftly. And with calculated-precision they had the benz surrounded within seconds... Moments later, they opened-fire on them relentlessly. Then paused after 30 seconds, tossing the lit homemade molotoff cocktails inside... Then quickly resorted back to the gunfire, pumping several rounds into their burning bodies as they desperately tried to get out of the car...

Loud screams filled the night-streets as the brutal assault continued. Then only seconds later, tires were screeching, and the assassinated burning bodies was all that remained.

Police helicopters loomed over the area in eleven-minute intervals, with an active searchlight penetrating the radio'd location of the highly dangerous suspects. All they could see was the victims... The suspects were long gone.

****

Teflon was still extremely upset about Chuck getting over on him with the fake cocaine and spent everyday plotting on how he would punish him whenever he finally caught-up with him.

Nothing else mattered to him at this point. Revenge was heavy on his mind, and it wasn't long before he received a phone-call from one of his associates informing him that they spotted Chuck in a particular neighborhood... He told Shawn what was up, and they both stormed out the door, overly anxious for retribution.

Chapter 11

Ray Ray came to a slow stop in front of one of Teko's homes in Royal Oak Michigan on a black-n-gray 1300 Habussa motorcycle. He cut the bike off, then slowly rested it on the kickstand... He casually approached the five-foot-five-inch tall, middle-aged Spanish man known as Teko, after pulling off his helmet.

"Amigo." Spoke Teko as they shook hands and gave off a slight smile to one another.

"It's good to see you Ray Ray. Our mutual friend Smoke has never had a bad thing to say about you. And I'm honored that you trusted me enough to make my acquaintance today." Ray Ray just gave off a slight nod as a gesture of appreciation for Teko's warm reception.

As they went inside Teko's plush home, he offered Ray Ray a shot of Tequilla as he made one for himself... Ray Ray accepted the shot, then sat down on one of the barstool's at Teko's bar...

Teko laughed giddily as he focused on the large flat-screen television and listened to the news-report about a government shut-down that was looming because democrats and republicans couldn't come to an agreement concerning the national-deficit going forward.

Ray Ray looked at him curiously, then nonchalantly asked,

"Why you trippin' about that Teko, whussup?" Teko took a hefty swallow from the conac in his glass, then answered.

"Amigo, anytime there's a government shutdown, it always bring our worlds closer. People tend to see things differently when their bosses tell them to work without pay, despite them having families to feed. Like federal agents for instance. They tend too not take things so seriously when they feel betrayed by their bosses. That's when we approach them and let them know we don't operate like that. And as long as they remain loyal to us, we remain loyal to them. And if the world happened to stop spinning someday, their families would still never be left in the cold. I have a very loyal friend who is a federal DEA Agent. I've had him since the last government shutdown. I almost did time once when I tried to bribe him. But I got lucky and dodged that bullet on a technicality. Then a year later, a government shutdown happened. And after he saw how things played out with his constituents, it not only embarrassed him, it eroded his faith in the system entirely. And diminished his loyalty for them altogether. Here he was a patriot who put himself through school and joined the feds to make a difference in the world. And within the snap of a finger, here he was broke and couldn't function as a normal citizen. Couldn't feed his family and was in line at a soup kitchen... Needless to say, I received a phone-call from him shortly afterwards. Probably because having me as a friend instead of an adversary, made more sense at the time. And he's been a part of my family and underworld activities ever since... Now let's discuss what I truly called you over here to discuss... Amigo, as you already know, I am in the cocaine business. And I know how you feel about it, but I was hoping we could look pass that. And one of my main reasons for choosing you, is because Smoke told me that you are a practical thinker. And practicality combined with a ruthless nature, is the man I need for this job. And the way that Smoke defines you my friend, that man is you... So here's the situation... Whenever we transport our coke from overseas, it always comes with complications. You see amigo, the coast guards jack us for a mother-load every other year. It's covert of course, which means they will report one of the shipments. And use the other one to fulfill political agendas."

"Agendas like what?" asked Ray Ray curiously.

"Like having the funding to place certain politicians in position. 'Cause the better the position, the better their chances are of gaining more power and influence at the top level of the game. Amigo, every law that's changed or altered, is done for the soul purpose of attaining monetary leverage. It's always about the dollar at the end of the day. Because the one who usually has the most dollars, is usually the most effective... Now as for the business at hand, there will be two large shipments that's coming through from our friends overseas. One is supposed to get through, and one is not. One of the shipments is really a bunch of garbage-low-percentage stepped-on coke. And the other shipment is the real deal. But we have a little problem... There is a federal informant that will be on board one of the vessels. And he will attempt to give the authorities the co'ordinance and location of the vessels so they can seize both shipments... Your job is to assassinate him before that happens. If you agree to this assignment, we will meet again in two weeks to discuss it in more detail. And I will forever be indebted to you for this move that we stand to make over two-hundred-million dollars on... As well as gaining a critical edge over our competitors. And despite the way things may seem on the surface, always know that America's phony drug-game is a war that is only being fought in the minds of the people. It is at all times being fought with one hand and fed with the other. And these are facts my friend. Now with that being said, hopefully we will talk again soon, have a safe journey back home amigo."

Chapter 12

Two weeks later:

"Bogata Columbia will be the loading point. Then you will pass through Venezuala, and by the time you make it to Haiti, watch closely because our traitor will begin to alert his contacts before you reach the Dominican Republic. Because that is where they will try to hit the first shipment. But once that's taking place, I have guarantees from my government friend who will be in the company of Customs and Border Protection, that our real shipment will pass right through and safely end up in Miami. And we will take it from there. Comprende."

****

Brick had a distraught look on his face as he gritted his teeth and listened intently to the person on the other end... Moments later, he was flying out the door.

Brick pulled up to a location approximately twenty-minutes later, where the remnants of a violent shootout was evident as Tef's limp body laid sprawled-out on the concrete in a puddle of blood... Shawn was also slumped over the wheel in the black dodge-charger, with blood leaking profusely from his bullet-riddled body. There was another man laid-out a few feet away from Shawn and Tef. And Brick instinctively mumbled.

"He got one of them bitches," as he rushed over to him when he realized the dude was still alive. Brick leaned over the dude and said,

"I know it was Mr. A that sent you, but who else was with you. And who pulled the trigga on Tef?"

The dude had lost a lot of blood, and was hallucinating as the blood continued to ooze from the right side of his chest... Then out of the blue, the lil dude looked up at Adolph with bucked eyes as he swiftly entered their space while mouthin'

"Man, you ain't killed this nigga yet." Boh! Boh! Adolph allowed the two point-blank shots to his head to be the period to his sentence.

"Damn dawg, why you do that. I wasn't done talkin' to dawg." Brick asked in an angered tone.

"Man, fuck dawg. It wasn't shit else to talk to'em about. And that's the problem anyway. We been doin' too much talkin' to niggaz and not enough slumpin' they asses. That's why niggaz comin' at us like this in the first fuckin' place!"

Brick didn't even respond to Adolph. He just jumped in his ride and peeled off before the authorities got there.

Chapter 13

"Dawg, did you peep the move with Tef?" Brick asked Chop in a suggested tone.

"Whatchu mean dawg, what move?" Chop asked skeptically.

"Dawg, that nigga got hit wit' a fo-five, all body-shots. And them shits went straight through his vest.

"So, what about it?'

"Man, that shit wasn't spose' to happen with that brand of vest. And the nigga that sold'em to us put a guarantee'd stoppage of everything from a nine to a muthafuckin' AR on 'em."

Chop scratched the side of his dark-skinned face before responding.

"Damn dawg, straight-up?" Then he looked up at Brick and asked candidly,

"Who sold us them bitches dawg?" Brick poured himself a shot of Bacardi, then downed the entire glass straight with no chaser before he answered.

"It was that bitch-ass nigga Rocky man."

"So you mean to tell me, that nigga had us out here vulnerable in theses muhfuckin streets."

"It seems that way homie, but we won't know fasho until we holla at dat chump. So dawg, get dat nigga on the horn and tell'em we need to holla at'em ASAP. But don't spook'em. Make it seem like we need some more vest's or something."

"A'ight my dawg, I'm on it."

Chapter 14

As Rocky stepped from the F1-50 he'd pulled up in, he greeted Brick, Ray Ray, and Adolph as they all strolled to the backyard of the brickhouse on Ashland and Jefferson.

"Whuddup doe my nigg's, yall niggas wanna hit dis' blunt?" Rocky offered his smoke to them.

"Nah homie, we straight." Brick spoke up.

"You know how we get down. We get straight to bidness... Now dawg, about them vest you sold us, didn't you say they could withstand everthing from a 45 to a muhfuckin AR?"

"Fasho dawg, without a doubt."

"So you tellin' me you stand by that a hundred percent?"

"Fasho my dawg. The source I go through is government-connected. And dude been doin' this shit for years, he good."

Brick uttered a suggestion irritably before aggressively tossing one of the vest at his chest.

"Okay, well check this out dawg, slip that on and let's see what's poppin wit dem bitches foreal since you say ol' boy good."

Rocky hesitated and formed a puzzled expression before speakin' up nervously.

"Is all that really necessary my dawg?"

"Fuck yeah it's necessary nigga!" spat Adolph as he readily slapped a 45 bullet in the chamber of his weapon and shot a scornful look at Rock.

Rocky's movement became fidgety before he spoke-up in a jittery tone.

"Ay Brick, what part of the game is this dawg?"

"The same part of the game that got my nigga Tef up outta' here nigga. Now prove that them shits is A-1 nigga, and our beef is off the floor."

Rock sighed again as he scanned each one of the menacing faces that stared coldly back at him. Then reluctantly put the vest on...

Brick calmly instructed him to stand in front of a tree in the backyard they were standing in. Then Adolph eagerly took aim.

"Why you lookin' so nervous nigga. If it's all-good like you say it is, you good. You ready?" Adolph asked with a smirk after takin' a few sips from a styrophone cup.

Rock didn't answer, he just took a deep breath and said a silent prayer under his breath before the first shot rung out.

*"Lord please watch over-"Boh!...*Boh! Boh! Boh! Boh! ...As the force of the slugs knocked Rock into the tree, Brick upped the AR-15 that he'd loaded five rounds in, then instantly began firing rounds at his chest in unison with Adolph...

After the 45 and AR was empty, they casually strolled over to Rock's mangled body, and discovered that every bullet went through like a hot knife through butter. So at that point it was confirmed. The vests were definitely defected.

****

When police finally found Rock's partially decomposed body behind the abandoned house on the eastside of Detroit, his fingerprints confirmed that he was the man they were actively looking for ever since his name was mentioned in the fraudulent-vest investigation. Many of the vest's ended up in several police departments throughout Detroit. And was responsible for two officers getting killed in the line of duty because they had them on when a shootout ensued with a bank-robbery suspect. And the lack of protection from the generic

Loyalty Ain't Loyal Enough

Kevlar was ultimately attributed to the cause of their demise.

Chapter 15

As Brick walked in the Italian restaurant and sat down at the table with Ray Ray, his face displayed concern as he asked,

"Whuddup-doe my dawg, you sounded like somethin' was wrong over the phone. Is everything good?"

"Yeah homie, everything good. I just wanted to know if you game for shootin' a move with me out the country for a week or so. I gotta' knock a coupla' clowns head's off for my guy Teko. And it's a couple hundred Gs in it for us. One fa' you, and one fa' me. You wit' it?"

"Shiiiid my nigg, when we on that flight?"

"In a few days, so let yo' guys know to stay chill and hold down the fort until we get back."

"Fasho dawg. Oh, and check this out Ray Ray, do you think it's possible for me to get a nice plug on some work outta this?"

"Nah homie, cause this ain't got nothin' to do with no coke. This strictly a hit."

"Okay my dawg, I feel you. Well keep me posted fam, I'm still tryna get on A.S.A.P.

Ray Ray chose not to tell Brick all the details of the trip, because he knew that Brick's curiosity would cause him to seek more out of it, just as he did.

****

Adolph took a few sips from the styrophone cup in his hand before he spoke up.

"Check this out dawg, a nigga don't mean to sound insensitive-n-shit about the situation with Tef, but I told you I got a bitch on the team that's a beast on the cookin' tip. So whenever we get on, you need to let me show you what the bitch can do in the kitchen, foreal." Adolph made his pitch to Brick again.

Brick gave a slow nod then responded.

"We'a see dawg, we'a see."

Adolph shook his head in agreement, then offered Brick some of the promethazine mixed with strawberry crush soda.

"Dawg, you want some of my exotic pop?"

"Nah dawg, I'm straight. But good lookin."

"I got turned on to this bad-muhfucka here from my wild-ass cousin in Memphis. That nigga sip all day everyday."

"That's whussup." Brick never judged anybody for how they chose to get their mind right. He felt like your lane was your lane.

Chapter 16

When the cocaine-filled boat finally made it from Bogata Columbia to Venenzualla, Ray Ray watched Sergio pull out his cellphone and appear to be texting someone. He made a mental note, then focused on the mission... They cruised through Nicaragua, then made it to Haiti a short time later...

Ray Ray excused himself, then moments later, he slowly crept up behind Sergio as he was secretly communicating with his American DEA-contact via text messages. Ray Ray slothly wrapped his left arm around Sergio's neck, then brutally slammed the gold knife into his pumping heart...

Sergio kicked, jerked, and contorted violently for about eight seconds before his body grew weak in Ray Ray's tight grip... Ray Ray held fast on his death-grip, but before he completely stopped moving, Ray Ray calliously snatched the knife from his chest, then firmly pulled it across his throat as he was instructed too.

Sergio's body gave one last violent forward kick from his right leg, then fell limp in Ray Ray's arms as his cellphone dropped, and Ray Ray methodically lowered his body to the floor...

Ray Ray turned around and gave Brick a slight nod, then without hesitation, Brick pumped two slugs in Sergio's accomplice's head with the silenced Taurus nine-millimeter. His body hit the floor with a echoed thud, then Ray Ray and Brick swiftly dragged their bodies two feet away, placing them side by side.

Afterwards, Ray Ray casually pulled out a cellphone and dialed a number. A man with a heavy latin accent answered,

"Amigo." He spoke in spanish. Then Ray Ray responded as he was instructed too.

"Time is your friend."

"Ci." Said the man. Then the phone went dead.

Approximately ten minutes later, several Spanish and Haitian men entered the boat and swiftly retrieved the bodies. Then moments later a Spanish man approached Ray Ray to retrieve the gold, bloody knife.

Ray Ray didn't waist any time handing it over, then the man led them to the other boat where they waited with the authentic 5.2 metric-ton shipment of cocaine until they finally received the green-light to enter the Dominican Republic.

They made it through with ease due to most of the manpower being pre-occupied with the heavily diluted shipment. And by the time Sergio's federal contact realized that something went horribly wrong, it was too late and there was nothing he could do.

Chapter 17

As Chop downed another shot of the disbelief tequila, he proceeded to stuff more dollars into the G-string of the big-butt stripper as she did her dance routine to the song *'Where dem dolla's at'* by *Gangsta' Boo...* Chop cheered her on and yelled out,

"Make me give you all this shit baby. Work dat ass girl!" as he held up a stack of dollar bills. Chop was truly enjoying himself and made the stripper happy by the end of her session. And after downing a couple more shots of patron, and sitting through a couple more strippers, he decided to call it a night. But just as he was preparing to leave, he became transfixed on two separate locations of the club.

He quickly pulled out his phone and dialed Adolph's number in a hurry.

"Whuddup-doe Chop, what's poppin my dawg." Adolph answered.

"Shit my nigg, but peep game. I'm up at club exstacy, and you won't believe what two lames is up in this bitch right now."

"Who dawg?" Adolph asked with heightened curiosity.

"Dat bitch-nigga Dee-Dee, and that hoe-nigga Chuck."

"Whuudd. Keep them niggas on yo' radar dawg, I'm on my way."

Chop and Adolph laughed and made small talk as they left home-depot with four ten-gallon buckets, and other supplies...

By the time they made it to their designated location, it was dusk dark. Adolph laughed out loud as he watched Dee-Dee and Chuck squirm in the chairs they were tied too, with their feet resting inside buckets of liquid concrete.

"Ay Chop, look at these two bitch-made niggaz whimperin like lil hoes. One of'em a car-thief, and the other one a counterfeit drug-dealer."

Chop burst out laughin as he passed the blunt back to Adolph.

"Man I will be so glad when this damn concrete harden all the way up so we can go'head and push these niggaz off the pier and watch'em sink to the bottom of the muhfuckin Detroit river, ha ha"

121

Adolph continued to mock the situation as he pointed and poked his weapon against their blindfolds and duck-taped mouths...

Chuck and Dee-Dee cried and moaned as the fear grew in their hearts for what they felt was the inevitable.

--Several hours later, when they felt that the concrete was now sufficiently solid, Adolph walked over to Dee-Dee and mashed the rest of his Newport cigarette out on his face, then said,

"Okay you lil low-life bitch, you get to go first. And if you got any last words, save'em for God nigga, 'cause I don't wanna here dat shit. You shoulda' knew what the fuck you was signin'-up fo' when you stole my ride nigga."

Adolph placed the sig 45 against his temple, then fired... Boh! Boh! The first slug broke his neck, and the second one traveled through his left eye-socket, exiting the back of his head... Adolph gave his limp, bloody head a forceful slap with the pistol, then grabbed one side of the chair, as Chop grabbed the other side.

They both gave a forceful tug forward, then watched as Dee-Dee, the chair, and the concrete buckets that restricted his feet, went crashing into the water. They both laughed uncontrollably as they watched him sink slowly to the bottom of the river...

A few moments later, they waisted no time doing the same thing to Chuck. Only this time, Chop fired the two headshots that sealed Chuck's fate. Boh! Boh! They stood on the pier and smoked another blunt, as they watched the water until it settled... Then when they were comfortable with the fact that there were no visible mishaps, they casually climbed in a black Yukon and headed back to the hood.

As Chop and Adolph headed toward a safe house in the black Yukon, Adolph broke the silence after sipping from his styrophome cup.

"Dawg, I got a African dude who wanna be my plug on the heroin tip. He say he got some top-of-the-line dawg-food fa' da' streets that 'spose to be straight from Nigeria. So I'm 'bout to grab a ounce from dude to see if it's dat deal, then open up a few spots and watch dem bitches bang."

"Whatchu gon' call yo shit dawg?" Adolph sipped from his cup, then laughed before responding.

"Death row, nigga. Cause the mix that I'mma get dat bitch Anne to put on my shit, gon definitely flat line a few muhfuckas off the rip."

"Damn dawg, ol girl fuck wit' da dawg-food too?"

"Fuck yeah dawg, she grew up around nothing but fiends and dealers. And rightfully so, they passed the game on down. So watch this move bro, you know them fiends don't want that shit until it slump a few muhfuckas. Ha ha."

Chop laughed before responding.

"Make it happen then my-dawg. Is you gon' put Ray Ray and Brick down wit it?" Adolph laughed and sipped from the styrophome cup before answering.

"Fuck nah dawg. Fuck them niggas. This all me."

"Fasho my guy, I hear you, get yours."

Chapter 18

As Ray Ray and Brick rode down Gratiot Ave, Brick broke the silence as he gripped the stirring wheel.

"Dawg, so what did ol' boy Teko say about helpin you find Mr. Alverez bitch-ass?"

Ray Ray took a pull off the Newport before responding.

"He ain't say shit 'cause I didn't ask him."

"Why not?"

"Cause I can tell that he would be against me goin' at Mr. A's head."

"Oh yeah, even after that demo we put down for him on the boat?"

Ray Ray didn't answer so Brick continued.

"So how you gon' play it-"Brick suddenly paused as he squawked-

"Hell nah, dawg look!" ...When Ray Ray looked around, he couldn't believe he was looking at Mr. Alverez climbing in the backseat of a silver Bentley.

125

They both immediately perked-up and followed him a short distance until his driver pulled up in a drive-thru car wash.

Brick swiftly pulled up on the exit end of the car wash... Ray Ray hurriedly rushed to the trunk and retrieved the sig 45 and handed it to Brick, then positioned the AR-15 under his arm...

The moment Mr. Alverez's driver pulled out of the car wash and stopped at the street-entrance, waiting for a break in traffic, Ray Ray and Brick approached the Bentley from opposite sides as they aggressively opened fire on it...

A startled Mr. Alverez spilled his drink as he instantly threw his hands up in surrender. But after approximately 40 rounds was fired between both guns, Mr. Alverez managed to regain his composure only seconds later... Snapping back to the realization of the bullet-proof doors and windows on the vehicle he was riding in... He sat up straight, then smiled at Ray Ray as he waved his finger as a gesture of 'not this time fellas,' then jerked out of view as the Bentley accelerated into traffic at a high-speed.

"Damn!" squawked Ray Ray as he and Brick trotted to their vehicle and left the scene in a hurry.

Two weeks later:

The moment that Adolph and Chop pulled up on an eastside block in the grand- boulevard area, Adolph focused on the three dudes that sat on the porch of a single flat, drinkin' 40 ounces of Colt 45, and re-directing customers from Adolph's spot to their's.

…. after another 45 minutes had passed, Adolph casually spoke to Chop in a calculated tone.

"My nigg, you know what's so tripped-out about growin' up in the hood?"

"What's that dawg?"

"Most of the time it's dawg-eat-dawg out here… And sometimes these streets can turn a nigga into becoming a muhfuckin' homicidal maniac out this bitch when it comes to niggas steppin' on toes about dat fettuchini. Ha ha." Adolph smirked as he twirled the wood toothpick around in his mouth and exited the vehicle. He casually walked down to their spot with a plastic bag in hand that came from a grocery store.

"Whuddup doe my nigg's… question… Is yall niggas responsible for this raw on the block with Hussein stamped on it?"

A skinny dude with long dreads spoke up first.

"Fasho my dude, that be us. Best shit on the streets fasho... Yo Marv, let me holla atchu right quick." He motioned for a known fiend named Marv to come up on the porch they were on. Once Marv entered their space, he casually handed Marv a pack of the heroin with Hussein stamped on it, then spoke-up.

"Here nigga, don't worry about mainlinin' that shit, just take it to the dome and blow it right quick so I can show dawg what it's hittin' fo'." Marv anxiously opened the pack, then looked around at the occupants dumbfoundedly before asking-

"One of yall got a dolla-bill I can borrow right quick?" Dread-head gave him a dolla then mouthed,

"Gimee my muhfuckin' dolla back when you finish nigga." The dopefiend rolled up the dolla-bill, then stuck it inside the pack and took a hard snort up each nostril....

A few moments later, he began scratching his arms in slow-motion, talkin' about how A-1 it is, then fell into a heavy-nod in mid-sentence... All of the men on the porch burst-out laughin at how the fiend still held his balance in the middle of his nod.

"Need I say more my nigg?" Dread-head spoke-up with confidence.

Adolph shook his head in approval before responding.

"Okay Okay, that's whassup my dawg. But check this out homie. The only reason I fell thru is to let yall niggas know, dat Hussein shit gotta' slide to another block, 'cause this my shit dude."

"You talkin' 'bout that Deathrow garbage nigga?" Dread-head responded aggressively.

"Fuck yeah nigga! So pack yall bags my dude. I insist!" Adolph squawked back.

"Suck my dick nigga!" Dread-head stood up in defiance.

Adolph instantly spat back.

"Suck mine first bitch!" -boh!

The hollow-point slug that ripped thru Dread-heads penis caused him to instantly clutch his groin area and yell out in pain. —boh! The second slug that tore thru his forehead caused him to violently hit the porch face-down.

"Now you other two bitch-niggas get the fuck up... Drag that bitch in the house, now!" The other two men did as they were told. And once they were inside, Adolph made them lay face downside by side. —Boh! Boh! —Boh! Boh! Adolph gave each man two bullets to the back of their heads, then reached inside the plastic-bag and retrieved the three Molotov cocktails... He lit each one and tossed them amongst the three bodies, then casually walked out pass the dopefiend who was still engaged in a heavy nod on the front porch. —When the fire department finally showed up to battle the heavy flames, they held the dopefiend there until the police arrived and arrested him as the primary suspect for the arson. Adolph blasted the song entitled *'Kill'em All'* by Twista as him and Chop slowly pulled off from the scene.

Chapter 19

By the time Teko heard about the attempt on Mr. Alverez's life, he was calling Ray Ray's phone every hour on the hour...

When Ray Ray finally answered, Teko stated in an agitated tone,

"Ray Ray, we need to talk." Then he insisted that they meet somewhere immediately.

A few hours later:

-Teko approached Ray Ray with a firm handshake and a odd smile before speaking.

"Sometimes in life my friend, it's far more better to make intelligent moves, than to make courageous moves. Because getting emotional when someone has wronged you, will only cause you to make critical mistakes somewhere down the line. Now with that being said, let me say this. I can't stress to you enough how proud you've made me and my associates with the professionalism you displayed while engaging the mission on the vessel. You truly put us on a seriously different level of strength. And now, we are stronger than ever, and plan to remain that way. In all of my years of being in this game, I've never introduced anyone to my employer. But if you truly want to assassinate Mr. Alverez, there will be a mandatory meeting for you to meet him, (After the job is done.) Why? Because Mr. Alverez has made a substantial amount of money for our organization during the many, many years we've been dealing with him. And there is absolutely no way you can kill him without assuming his position in its entirety... Meaning, all of his customers, will become your customers. All of his territory will become your territory. And the two- hundred million dollars he's worth, will suddenly be your worth. And let me also stress that there is no way around this ordinance. Or the full force of my organization will automatically be against you Ray Ray, and there's nothing that I'd be able to do to change it." Teko paused for a few intense seconds to let the seriousness of his statement sink in, then continued.

"Ray Ray, as I stated before, I'm fully aware of your stance on drug-dealing. And I notice how you cringe and frown upon the mere mention of it. This thing has been eating at you for years. And the way I see it, it's mainly because you were truly too young to identify with what you were actually dealing with... In your mind, you thought you'd developed a hate for drug-dealers, when in all actuality, you only developed a hate for bad businessmen, period. And I get it, I know that your heart will always be driven by your hood-instincts, and that's okay. It was a part of your beginning and will ultimately be a part of your end. But the only thing left for you to do now, is understand this. What unites us, is so much bigger than what divides us... So, if assassinating Mr. Alverez is the one thing that's going to unite us, by all means, do what you must do. Then prepare to embrace your new position wholeheartedly. Now, is there anything that you want to add before we conclude this discussion."

Ray Ray rubbed his head peevishly before responding.

"I hear ya' dawg, I hear ya. But check this out, if my memory serves me correctly, when my boy Smoke was alive, ain't you da' one who showed him flicks of what that piece'a shit Deo look like so he could get at'em?"

"Yes Amigo, that's a fact. But that's an entirely different scenario. The contract was already inked for Deo. And besides, sometimes to win on a certain level, a queen has to sacrifice a pawn... Now with that being said, I have nothing more to add to this inquisition. The terms have been laid out and they are what they are. In the meantime, we will be intouch my friend... Adios."

Chapter 20

After Sheila finished making popcorn for Myonly, Love, and lil Ray, she yelled in the bathroom and asked Ray Ray did he want a turkey sandwich.

"Yeah bae, hook me one up too." He answered back.

"Okay!"

Sheila strolled to the kitchen, washed her hands, then began her food prep... She was interrupted moments later when the land-line phone rung... She placed the wheat bread on the counter then answered cordially.

"Hello."

"Sheila, don't hang up, because your life depends on it." The caller warned.

"Who the fuck is this?" Sheila asked with conviction.

"My name is officer Smitty Branch. I'm sure you've probably heard of me."

Sheila paused for a moment at the mention of his name, then spoke up again.

"Well what do you want?"

"Good question baby. I want the world and everything in it, but for now I'll just settle for your cooperation,"

"And what da' fuck that 'spose to mean?"

"Ha Ha Ha- it means that if you don't, you die."

"You listen up you pig muthafu- "

"Aut Aut Aut! I suggest you listen to the odds before you get all cocky on me bitch. Now the first thing you need to do is look out the living-room window of that big pretty house of yours."

Sheila stormed to the living room and glared out the window with an intense focus... Officer Branch gave a short wave as he leaned against his cranberry Crown Vick.

Sheila was instantly startled at the sight of him and quickly backed away from the window.

"Now I want you to go look in your refrigerator." He instructed contently. Sheila slowly walked over to the fridge and opened it up.

"Now slowly slide the half-gallon of milk to the side."

Sheila was hesitant, but she did it." –The first thing she saw was a half of a donut laying on a small saucer. Then her heart began to thump rapidly as the

136

dangerous-looking bundle of dynamite wrapped in black tape, connected to a timer with visible red –n-blue wires, came into view.

"Uh!" Sheila covered her mouth to muffle the panicky sigh she'd just released.

"Ha ha ha. Do you sound like that because of the donut I didn't finish, or because of the new understanding we have?" Sheila didn't answer.

"Well, I feel that you should know that I'm a man who likes to be clearly understood. So now I want you to walk over to the cabinet and remove the family-size box of fruit-loops." -As Sheila removed the box of cereal, her breathing intensified as she stood there staring at another explosive-device identical to the one in the refrigerator.

"Now, there's four more devices like that placed throughout the house. And if you don't do as I say, I will hit the button on this little gadget in my hand and incinerate that muthafucka, early. Is that understood?... I can't hear you. I said is that understood!"

"Ye- yes." Sheila answered nervously.

"Yes what?"

"Yes, it's understood." She mumbled in a defeated tone.

"Okay, now here's the deal. There are five of you muthfuckas in the house right now. But only four of you will walk the fuck out. And I want you to know that it's mandatory for you to be one of the people that come out, or everybody dies. You got five minutes to make it happen bitch, the clock is ticking."

The perception of the shrewd cop quickly engulfed Sheila's mind as she realized the sordid game he'd propagated. She was utterly disgusted at the audacity of the snake-muthafucka and was seriously afflicted because she had no time to resolve it. The moment Sheila and the kids were out of the house and a few meters down the road in her car, Officer Smitty Branch lit a cigarette as he displayed a sinister grin, then coldly whispered-

"By by bitch, it's been real." He casually pressed the button on the connecting device in his hand... Booom!! –Crack-Boooom!!

The explosive was massive, and the force that it produced blew the house to pieces. Officer Branch was truly elated, and he prayed that Ray Ray's death was horrifically painful.

A sense of relief and redemption rushed over him because he felt that this was finally a closed chapter in his life. He tightly-gripped the steering wheel, all smile's as he slowly pulled away from the carnage left behind.

Meanwhile, as Sheila drove down the road with the children highly distraught, she couldn't believe how they allowed the piece-of-shit cop to get the ups on them and force her to display a form of disloyalty towards her man that she never thought was possible. Nevertheless, she remained optimistic, and prayed that things would manifest in their favor. Her nervous stomach formed knots in it as each second ticked by. And a consistent flow of tears rushed down her troubled face.

She repeated a series of prayers about the situation in its entirety, then made a personal vow to never give up on trying to wipe Smitty off the face of the earth... She silently stressed to herself that the retribution would be brutal. Because she without-a-doubt wanted him to die in the worst way.

-Brick hung up the phone frustrated again because it was his fifth time calling Ray Ray that day with no answer.

-Sheila was elated when Ray Ray finally showed up at their designated spot, with only a few minor burns but was otherwise alright.

Ray Ray reflected back to the text message that Sheila sent him telling him about the threat that they were facing with officer Smitty. Which allowed them to immediately put a plan in motion. It was truly ironic that Ray Ray actually purchased that particular house because it had a built-in wine-cellar that was a fortified bomb-shelter as well. The previous owner was a conspiracy theorist. And with time and money on his side, he made an addition to his home that complimented the way he viewed the world.

Ray Ray felt that it turned out to be the perfect house considering the circumstances. Or he surely would've been a dead man.

After pulling himself together, he immediately linked-up with Brick and informed him on the unexpected drama with Smitty. Then regained his composure shortly afterwards and got back focused on their missions going forward.

Chapter 21

"Sss, hmm, ssshmm bay-bee... oow, oh yeah. Yes baby. Just like that. Get this pussy baby. Get it." Syann was in a pure erotic zone as the Caucasian female known as Snow-Magic worked her unusually thick, long tongue inside Syann's soaked pussy.

The Caucasian female earned the nickname Snow Magic solely because of her gifted tongue. And those who got a chance to experience it fell head over heels in lust with it. Snow knew exactly what to do with it and would purposely try to turn any broad out who gave her the opportunity to work it.

She was also a petite gorgeous female with soft feminine features. But the way she worked her skillful tongue, caused her to feel like a roughneck-burly broad...

Syann would always close her eyes tightly and imagine Ray Ray sexing her whenever Snow would get to the point where she was literally penetrating her hole as if she was doing it with a real penis. The seven inches of firm tongue had Syann climbing up the walls, as it consistently slithered in and out in a steady rhythm, then periodically flicked her clitoris in every direction.

"Ahhhh! Ooh shit baby! You doin' it! You doin' it baby!" Syann felt herself about to explode at any moment. And Snow knew she had her victim on the ropes.

"Ooooh, I'm cu, I'm cu, Ray Ray, I'm- "Snow didn't care about Syann calling out a man's name during their times of sexing, she was all for it... Just when she felt Syann was on the brink of exploding, she added to the sensation by inserting two lubricated fingers in Syann's asshole.

Syann yelled out-

"ooooh- fuuuuuuck! As she began violently jerking and convulsing. A heavy load of cum sprayed Snow's face as it aggressively shot out of Syann's throbbing hole....

Snow continued to work her fingers as she simultaneously licked, sucked, and slurped up any trace of cum she could find.

"Syann's face and body was so tensed up as Snow worked her magic, then she suddenly relaxed entirely

to the point that she could've passed out at any moment.

Snow made her way up to Syann's open mouth, then leisurely twirled her cum-soaked tongue around her lips and tongue. The kisses were deep, passionate, and sensuous, and Snow toyed with Syann's pink protruding nipples as the session came to a slow close. –Syann took a shower then went to the phone and called her cousin Oeekwa.

-As Oeekwa and her male friend Dawhite sat in the hotel room they'd spent the night in, Oeekwa began to feel a little guilty for not allowing Dawhite to come to her home yet... She had a three-year-old son who was about to turn four in one week. And she vowed to herself that she would not have different men in and out of his space until she was a hundred percent sure about whatever man she was involved with. Her son's biological father was in state prison serving 30 years for a homicide. And Dawhite would always assure her that he was the man for her, and would often complain about the fact that they'd been dating for almost a year with little progress...

Dawhite felt that it was time to cross that threshold and allow him to meet her son. But Oeekwa explained to him that she wasn't quite ready.

As they were finishing up the Chinese food that they ordered, Oeekwa asked Dawhite to excuse her when she saw the prison number come across her cellphone.

"This is a federal prison, from-"

"Syann."

"Press five to accept this call, or-" Oeekwa cut the recording short by pressing the five as she stepped in the bathroom for some privacy.

"Whuddup doe cousin." Syann spoke excitedly.

"Shit couz, same ol same ol, what's poppin with you girl."

"Shit. I was just callin' to see if you was scoopin' up my lil man for lil Twan's birthday party?"

"Yup, I talked to dawg and he said I could get him one more time. But after this time it would be a minute because his world is a little chaotic right now."

Syann sighed momentarily before responding.

"Girl since when is that nigga world not chaotic. He may have to rethink that shit because that means I won't get a chance to see him on my next visit."

"Well girl I don't know what's what with that. I'm just tellin' you what he told me... Anyhow, you just make sure you call me bright and early on Twan's birthday so you can wish my baby a happy-b-day and talk to lil Ray cause he was tellin me he missed his mommie the last time I spoke to him."

"Girl don't tell me that, cause you know I will come up outta this bitch and be at the muhfuckin party with mines." Syann spoke emotionally.

"Oh yeah," Oeekwa asked in a jovial manner.

"Well I'll see you there gottdamit."

"Don't light the candles without me, shiiid." They both burst out laughing. Then talked a little more before the fifteen-minute call ended...

When Oeekwa exited the bathroom, Dawhite had a funny look on his face as if something heavy was on his mind, then he nonchalantly spoke up.

"Ay babe, not to be in yo' bidness or nothing, but was you just talkin' to a chick name Syann?" Oeekwa paused for a moment before she answered him because she knew the *'nosey muthafucka'* had to be eavesdropping to ask a question like that.

"Yeah, Syann is my first cousin, why, whassup?"

"I used to know a chick name syann who use to strip. She was light-skinned, tattoos, with one on her leg that says *'How Many Licks.'*"

Oeekwa abruptly cut him off...

"Yeah that's her, dude don't tell me you use to fuck her."

"Nah Nah, it wasn't nothin' like that. My boy use to holla at'er." He lied. Then fell into a quiet state of reflection about the *night that she set him up to be beaten and robbed for the five kilos and the hundred-*

145

grand. *He became highly anxious in his being because he knew for a fact that he heard Oeekwa say Syann was going to be at her son's b-day party. And he made a mental note that he couldn't miss it for nothin' in the world.*

Chapter 22

Ever since Syann had went to prison, Ray Ray would drop his son off to her cousin Oeekwa every other month because Oeekwa would always take lil Ray up to visit with Syann. Nevertheless, Sheila hated the arrangement, but she kept quiet about it because she knew how Ray Ray was when he had his mind made up about something. He only allowed the visits because he was impressed with the fact that Syann didn't snitch him out to the feds. Knowing she could've easily used him as a get-out-of-jail free card but didn't. So he felt that allowing her to see her only child every so often was the least he could do to show his appreciation... And despite all of the recent chaotic events, he felt that he would let them visit with him one more time, then put it on hold for awhile until he could figure some things out...

As Ray Ray and his son sat in his car at the park waiting for him to be released to Oeekwa, Ray Ray took the time to share a few words with him as he always did.

"Alright my guy, you know the drill. Walk over to the sliding-board and stand there until your aunt Oeekwa come get you. I'll be right here until she's holding your hand, alright?"

"Okay daddy."

"Now before you go, what did daddy always say you're suppose to do out here in society?"

The bright-eyed three-year old looked up at Ray Ray and spoke with a hint of confidence.

"Daddy, you said stay two steps ahead of sucka's. And four steps ahead of lames." Ray Ray let out a proud laugh as he rubbed his head and responded.

"That's right my guy, that's definitely our approach. And daddy's so proud of the way that you retain that information."

Ray Ray gave him a gentle hug when he noticed Oeekwa standing over by the slide.

"Alright my guy, take care, and I'll see you in a week. I love you man."

"I love you too daddy."

Lil Ray stepped out of the car and made his way over to the slide as he was instructed too. Then about ten minutes later, he was hand in hand with Oeekwa...

She gave Ray Ray an inconspicuous nod, then blended in among the other children until she felt that there was no threat in the area and was comfortable enough to get in her vehicle and pull off.

Chapter 23

As Ray Ray sat outside of the Catholic church, he reflected on many of the recent activities that transpired in his life up to this point. He thought about how Teko held up to his end of the deal and paid him ten million dollars for the job... He also thought about the serious discussion that he had with Teko about the terms of assassinating Mr. Alverez. Ray Ray fully understood that Teko was a highly intellectual individual. And was officially seasoned when it came to reverse psychology. He could read the character of a man by just being in his presence for a mere ten minutes. And could call things out about the man as if he was a criminal profiler. Ray Ray also knew that nothing was ever (by-chance) with Teko. Like the time he mentioned the fact that Mr. Alverez attended church every Sunday no matter what. And that nine times outta' ten, there would be a celebrese woman with him everytime.

Ray Ray knew that Teko provided that information to him deliberately. It was a direct symbolic challenge, nothing less than bait to see if Ray Ray would bite because he knew first-hand how uncomfortable Ray Ray was with the terms of the assassination… Ray Ray saw right through it but he didn't take any offense to it because whatever fate the future held, Ray Ray felt that he was the navigator of his own destiny regardless of what another gangster said.

Ray Ray's thoughts subsided and his heartbeat sped-up. The sudden surge of anxious adrenaline shot through his body the moment he saw Mr. Alverez and the Celebrese woman emerge from the church. Ray Ray was dressed as if he was also a church-attendee. Wearing a dark gray Bruno Armani suit, gray gators, and a black-n-gray dob hat encased in a black silk band. He waited impatiently in the short distance as Mr. A in company, made their way to their vehicle. Mr. A's bodyguard was close by his side. So Ray Ray knew from the last encounter that he couldn't let Mr. A make it inside the bullet-proof car. He moved in a slow, methodic pace as he slid in their space undetected… Tightly gripping the silencer-tipped ten-shot sig with an extended thirty-round clip… The first person he made eye contact with was the Celebrese woman. Which instantly caused her to place a hand over her open mouth in a frantic state and yell *Devil* in Spanish.

"Diablo! Diablo!"

Boh! boh! boh! boh! Ray Ray let off four quick shots at the burly bodyguard first. Two in his stomach, and two in his face... Then focused on Mr. Alverez as they locked eyes for what seemed like eternity.

"Winning is the name of the game Ray Ray. And for every champ, there is always a contender. And I must admit, I underestimated your approach to the *Art of War.* But you did very well my friend. And turned out to be a formidable opponent, worthy of serious regard." Mr. Alverez spoke his last words with a tone of honor. And in that light, Ray Ray respected it. He pushed the weapon closer to Mr. A to finish him, but just before he squoze the trigger, the words of Teko hyper-flashed through his mind,

"It wasn't drug-dealers that you hated Ray Ray. It was bad businessmen."

Boh! boh! boh! boh! boh! - By the time the Celebrese woman opened her eyes from the silent-prayer she'd mumbled over and over, the cold-hearted assassin was long gone... And the bullet between Mr. Alverez's eyes, the bullet that was lodged in his throat, and the two that opened up his chest cavity followed by the breathless gasp, was the validation that Mr. Alverez was no longer among the living.

Chapter 24

Dawhite exhaled the smoke from the Newport cigarette he held as he sat in a stolen car across the street from Oeekwa's house, reflecting on the day he followed her home. He marveled at the fact that she was none-the-wiser and snickered out loud as he intently loaded the semi-automatic carbine rifle. -----

-Happy birthday to you, happy birthday to you, happy birthday dear Twan. Happy birthday to you. — Boh! boh! boh! boh! boh! boh! boh! boh! boh! boh! –

The bullets that tore through the house left an array of chaos and blood-curdling screams... In the aftermath, Oeekwa lay shot in the leg. And one of her son's friends lay shot in the arm. But the most tragic of the bunch was little Ray, as he lay lifeless from the four bullets that ripped through his small frame. It was a horrific display of misfortune. And things would only get deeper from this point forward.

-Syann immediately dropped the phone as she screamed to the top of her lungs. She momentarily looked around frantically, then abruptly attacked the closest female inmate to her. It was a Spanish female who she'd already had words with before about taking too much time cooking her food in the microwave. The issue was that Syann was trying to cook a three-minute bag of popcorn in between the Spanish chick's hour-long meal. And the Spanish chick said no, and Syann didn't appreciate it. And she made a mental note that she would clown on the chick if they ever had any more words... Syann was devastated about her deceased son as she violently pummeled the lady. Using him as an excuse to do what she wanted to do to her anyway... The correctional officers tackled Syann aggressively, taking her to the floor hard. Then handcuffed her and whisked her off to the segregation unit, also known as the hole. Syann couldn't believe something like that happened to her child. And even though she was extremely crushed about her baby, she was equally crushed about the fact that she may lose contact with Ray Ray forever. And just the thought of that had her more mentally unstable.

Chapter 25

As Valerie Gates stood at the podium among family, friends, and spectators at her younger brother's funeral, she repeatedly scanned the room as if she was eagerly looking for someone as she concluded her speech about him.

"We gotta' stop all this killin each other yall, foreal." She wiped a fresh tear and glanced around at the crowd sincerely before continuing.

"My baby brother was only nineteen years old. And his life is fuckin' over."

The black heavyset reverin in attendance slightly cringed when he heard the curse word.

"My brother was killed for hangin' with the wrong muthafuckin' crowd, and it ain't shit in this wicked ass world that's gon' bring him the fuck back. Fuck this shit yall! I'm so tired of this stupid, ass, shiiit!" She was now yelling to the top of her lungs as the

Paul barrers alongside the reverin closed in on her to bring the sermon to a hault.

"Back the fuck up offa' me. I ain't done yet gottdamit!" She yelled at them as she continued her rant.

"And the sad part about all of this shit, is that there will most certainly be more premature funerals after this one. 'Cause the very second that I find the muthafuckas that did this shit to mine, them bitches is dead! Do you fuckin' hear me, dead!"

The reverin had heard enough at this point, so he moved in close to her and reached for the microphone.

"I hear you sister, and most importantly God hears you. But this is not the way to honor your loved one. So please have a seat and try to calm down."

Valerie stared at him momentarily in defiance, ready to slap him silly if he touched the mic... But only moments later, she relaxed her demeanor and gave in when one of her aunties in the front row spoke up.

"Val, we hear you baby, now come sit beside me so we can bury Eric properly and figure some things out, please baby."- Valerie broke down in tears again as she handed the reverin the microphone and submitted to her aunt's request.

--The service lasted 45 minutes longer, then Eric's body was driven to the cemetery on eight-mile-n-Vandyke where he was finally put to rest.

Chapter 26

When the meeting concluded with Teko and his organization, Ray Ray walked out of there as one of the most powerful underworld bosses in the United States. He now had Italians, Russians, and Columbians as customers. And controlled 65 percent of all the cocaine entering the United States.

-He speed-dialed Sheila's phone as soon as he got in the car, because she'd texed him the words *'Call me A.S.A.P baby, something terrible has happened.'*

When Ray Ray finally heard the news about his only son, the numbness and grief that fell over him was unbearable. He sunk into a deep state of depression and dropped his head in defeat as he sat inside the brand-new bullet-proof Bugatti (that was a gift that most new bosses received,) shedding tears for hours. And even though he was rocked to the core of his being, he was still a realist. And was always aware of the fact that heavy games often bred heavy consequences. And he felt that more-than-likely, it was just another round of karma that had just unmercifully touched his world... As Raynard Thompson combed through the heavy reflections of his complicated life, he never in a million years thought he'd see the day when he'd become a full-fledged cocaine dealer. But overall, he came to grips with the situation, and made up his mind to put all his past phobias behind him and fully fall in line with the spirit of the organization, then find the people responsible for his son's demise and punish them accordingly. He had a heart-to-heart discussion with Brick, letting him know that he was fully connected now, and that he was officially Brick's new plug. Then handed him a duffle-bag that contained a hundred kilos of the best coke that money could buy. Then he explained to Brick how his role would eventually get bigger in the organization as time went forward. Brick was ecstatic and could hardly contain himself. He was a drug-dealer at heart, and never desired to be anything else... He wholeheartedly took Ray Ray's advice when he advised him to spoon-feed Adolph, and never reveal to him exactly how much weight he could get his hands on at any given time. Because Adolph was predictable, yet unpredictable in the same breath.

Brick gave Adolph some work, and also allowed his contact-person crack-head Anne to be their new chef. It turned out to be a smooth arrangement, and the money began to flow in better than old times. −Brick grabbed the keys to his truck from his pocket as he prepared to leave the safe-house... He walked toward the kitchen where Anne was hooking up some work but stopped abruptly when he noticed her sitting in a chair sucking Adolph's dick as Adolph stood in front of her. Adolph noticed Brick's presence, so he looked back with a smile as he exhaled the weed smoke and said.

"Dawg, you gotta' get you one of these demo's in yo' life one day nigga. This bitch is just as skillfull on a dick as she is cookin up the work. I'm tellin you nigga."

Brick smirked and replied,

"You silly nigga." Then walked out the door to go meet up with Ray Ray's new arms dealer.

Chapter 27

After shaking hands with the middle-aged Hispanic man, Brick listened attentively as the man went over the merchandise with him.

"Okay my friend, this weapon here is called a Sturmgewehr 44 assault rifle. The country of its origin is Germany. The caliber is 7.92x33 mm. The overall length is 37 inches. Cartridge capacity is 30 rounds. Muzzle velocity is approximately 2,133ft. Effective range, 546 yards. Rate of fire, 500 rounds per minute." He casually moved to the next weapon.

"Now this one here is the 1903 springfield bolt-action rifle. It's nick-named *Silent Death*, because if you hear it fire, you're already dead. The caliber is 30-06. Cartridge capacity is 5 rounds. Rate of fire, ten rounds per minute."

Brick smiled before he continued.

"This one here is a FN-FA1. Holds 20 rounds. Performance-wise it produces 650-700 rounds per minute. I call it the truth because it's true to the job it says it does... This next one is a weapon that helped win World War 2. It's the M1 Garand. It's a stripper-clip feed. Holds 8 rounds. And does not jam. A true showstopper for sure. Okay, now here we have a M-16. And this baby my friend, will prove it's worth on the battlefield. It performs at a 700 to 950 rounds per minute. And the 556-bullet tumbles when it's fired. I call it the rumble in the jungle, ha ha. Now this next one here is the Steyr Aug semi-assault rifle. It converts from a semi to a fully automatic. It was made in Austria. Cartridge capacity is 30 to 42 rounds per minute. It ejects shells on either side of the weapon, making it easier for left-handed shooters. It also has clear magazines to allow soldiers to see how many rounds are left. It has an interchangeable barrel-system, and because it's a short weapon, it's very combat-effective in close-quarters. This one definitely gets my vote of confidence amigo."

By the time the man had finished his presentation, Brick was super impressed. And he knew that dude was without-a-doubt the real deal. Brick purchased everything that was presented to him and more, under Ray Ray's instructions. He also bought BMG armored piercing insindiary rounds, along with thirty AK 47's, because dude labeled AK's his number one weapon for combat.

Chapter 28

Weeks after lil Ray was laid to rest, the streets finally provided Ray Ray with an address for DaWhite...

"Please! Please don't kill us!" squawked DaWhite's mother as Ray Ray, Brick, and Adolph stood in her living room with guns drawn. Adolph gripped a handful of her hair and yelled.

"Shut up bitch before I slump yo' dumb ass on the strength." Then he yanked her head close to his face and grimmed her hard as he glanced around the room.

Ray Ray casually walked up to her and spoke in a deliberate tone.

"Listen up lady, cause I'm only gonna say it once. Get your phone and call your son DaWhite if you wanna live. And is anybody else in this house with you that I should know about?"

DaWhite's mother hesitated before answering. Then she quickly contemplated whether she should gamble on not telling them that DaWhite's girlfriend was hiding in the closet. But the fear that gripped her mind and body, wouldn't allow her to withhold any information that might get her killed, so she blurted out.

"Okay, I'll call DaWhite, but please don't hurt his girlfriend that's hiding in the bedroom closet." Adolph's demeanor changed when he heard mention of DaWhite's girlfriend. And he quickly pushed DaWhite's mother to Brick, then rushed to the bedroom to find her.

A few moments later, DaWhite answered his mother's phone call just as Adolph emerged from the bedroom with his pregnant girlfriend.

"Whassup ma." His voice transmitted over her speaker phone, then Ray Ray spoke up instead.

"Yo DaWhite, check this out my man. Here's the deal. You can do one of two things. You can come home immediately and save yo moms and ol lady. Or you can turn ya'self in at the nearest precinct, it's on you."

"Who da' fuck is this." Spat DaWhite.

"Bitch nigga don't worry 'bout who da' fuck it is. Just get yo bitch-ass over here or turn yo'self the fuck in like dawg said or you can listen to me fuck the shit outta yo momma and yo bitch nigga." Adolph answered in place of Ray Ray.

"Man fuck yall niggas. I ain't doin' shit." DaWhite bucked.

"Okay nigga, you wanna play tough tone. I gotchu bitch." Adolph spoke angrily as he pulled DaWhite's mother close to him.

"Comeer bitch! Get on yo knees hoe. Get on yo muthafuckin knees!" He yelled too the top of his lungs as he unbuckled his pants and pulled out his dick. He aggressively rubbed it across her lips as she cried and attempted to turn away.

"Open yo mouth bitch! Open up before I slap all yo teeth out, then make you suck it wit' all gums bitch." DaWhite's mother cried out,

"For God's sake DaWhite, please turn yo'self in, please son, they serious."

"You gottdamn right we serious. Yo DaWhite, after yo mama suck my dick, I'ma fuck'er in da' ass man. What'chu gon' do nigga?"

DaWhite didn't answer.

"Damn moms, don't you wish you would've aborted that bitch-nigga. He 'bout to straight-up let you get ass-fucked before I put two holes in yo big ass head." Adolph shoved the head of his dick in her mouth, then laughed as she cried and tried to resist performing on him... Suddenly Adolph became overly

166

irate. He placed the barrel of the 9mm Ruger against her forhead.

"Okay bitch, playtimes over. I'm 'bout to blow yo' muthafuckin brains out the back of yo' head, you hear me bitch! All because yo coward-ass son kill kids."

"Noo! No! Please! I'll do whatever you want! Just please don't kill me!"

"It's too late bitch! It's too late! You outta' here hoe!" –

"Can I talk to any detective here. My name is DaWhite Walker, and I need to turn myself in for shooting up a house, killing an innocent little boy."

Ray Ray immediately gave the signal for Adolph to stop once he heard DaWhite's voice come over his mother's phone... In the background you could hear several walkie-talkie transmissions, along with what sounded like genuine police conversations with DaWhite. An aura of relief swept over the room as everybody came to the realization that he'd really just turned himself in. And just like that, the ordeal had came to an end, so it seemed.

After Ray Ray and Brick exited the front door, Adolph stepped out last. He suddenly stopped, then casually turned around and stepped up to DaWhite's 8 month pregnant girlfriend. His menacing expression let it be known that something sinister was on his mind, as he coldly pressed the barrel of the nine against her swollen belly- boh! boh! boh! boh! boh! boh! boh!

"You kill ours; we kill yours bitch. Flat out." Then he smirked at her sprawled-out body on the floor as he fled the scene with Ray Ray and Brick... Under normal circumstances, Ray Ray would've flipped out about a move like that. But the present day in time had his feelings on ice. He didn't properly know how to process sentiment. And found himself consistently numb towards things he would've otherwise been emotional about... In his mind, he simply charged it to the game.

Chapter 29

As Val pulled up to the Chinese restaurant on telegraph and 6 mile, her heart dropped when she noticed Adolph already coming out with food in hand. Brick sat on the driver-side of the silver Escalade as Adolph climbed in on the passenger side... Adolph opened the bags to make sure the order was right, and never even noticed the fast-approaching Valerie who was at the Escalade mouthing off within seconds, after aggressively banging on the window.

"Oh, so you too good to answer a bitch phone-calls nigga?" Adolph and Brick both looked up at the same time.

"Nigga I haven't heard from you since my brother Eric got killed fuckin' with you. And not only did you not pay for his funeral, you didn't even come to the muthafuckin funeral. You foul nigga." She banged on the window some more.

"Roll down the muhfuckin window dude and face me like the real nigga you claim to be. You know I know the whole scoop on yo' punk ass! Yall went at them niggas simply because you wanted yo' crack-head ass mama to be the chef instead of ol' boy" ----

"La, la la la, la la, la la la, la la, laaa, laaa, All you niggaz die!" Adolph abruptly turned up the volume on the radio blasting tupac's song entitled *"Trouble-Some",* to drown Val's voice out. Then he turned toward Brick and said...

"Pull off on this bitch dawg," Brick made a mental note of her license plate as they pulled off, because according to the little he could hear, there was definitely foul play on Adolph's behalf... And Brick planned to know just how foul it was.

Chapter 30

(Riiiiing-Riiiiiiiing)

"Hello."

"Whassup sexy, how you been?" Brick asked the woman on the other end.

"You would know how I been if you would've stayed in-touch Brick."

"Ah baby don't hold that against me. It's been a hectic past coupla' months for me, and my plate was off the charts with non-sense. But check this out, maybe we can grab a bite to eat tomorrow at outback, and wash it down with a smooth red wine, how 'bout it."

"Oh how tempting your offer sounds, but something tells me I should make you try a little harder, due to your lengthy absence with no effort to reach out to me in all that time."

"Come on Linda, where's your bleeding heart. Don't you know forgiveness is the key to all fresh starts."

"Is that right?"

"Most definitely, especially when you still like the person. Do you still like me baby?"

"I'm afraid to say yes because it might go to your head."

"Well Imma' take that as a yes regardless, and I'll see yo' fine ass tomorrow. Oh, by the way, are you still a police officer?"

"Detroit's finest, 6th precinct. Why do you ask?"

"Because I might wanna play with your handcuffs after we finish our meal."

"Still naughty huh?" She asked giddily.

"Just the way you like it slut. See you tomorrow."-*Click.*

****

...After Brick had the kind of savagely wild sex with officer Linda that she loved, he admired her shapely tight body as she slept peacefully in the kingsized bed on top of the blue satin sheets. She was brown-skinned, thick in all the right places, and as freaky as they come. Brick smiled to himself as he thought about how he'd convinced her to run Valerie's plate

172

number to get an address on her, then also provided him with an address for officer Smitty Branch.

He stared at her in the semi-darkness until he'd put out the blunt he was smoking... He made his way over to her and slid his hard flesh in her hot pussy while her ass was already tooted up. She instantly woke up letting out a soft grunt and moan, then reached back and pulled him closer as he massaged one of her supple breast and toyed with her rigid nipple as he picked up the pace on his forward thrust. He slid closer to her ear and whispered-

"Fuck da' police!" Then lustfully ran his tongue up the back of her neck as he gripped her tight and started pumping her wet flesh with a steady rhythm of intense strokes... Brick ravaged her again for another hour or so, then laid in the darkness in deep thought 'til he nodded off to sleep.

Chapter 31

"Brick, I remember the day that my brother left with Adolph. I had a seriously funny feeling, but I truly didn't know that it would be my last time seeing him. --- I overheard him telling my brother that they was goin' at some dude because they wanted Adolph's crackhead moma Anne to be the new chef instead of the dude. I think his name start with a T. I didn't even know that the bitch was his mother until one of my crack-head uncle's that use to smoke with her, told me the history. He knew Adolph's father too. He was a low-life wanna-be pimp that use to make her trick wit' different muhfuckas until he eventually o'deed one day. I guess Adolph is just like him 'cause he was foul as fuck too. And it makes me sick to my stomach that I was even fuckin' that cold-hearted bitch."

-Brick glanced over at Ray Ray as they processed everything Valerie had just revealed to them. And it was difficult for Brick to maintain his composure as his silent thoughts weighed on his mind.

"I'll be damned. That slimeball muthafucka killed my nigga Tef, then turned around and killed her brother Eric just in case he decided to tell me who pulled the trigger." Brick released a heavy sigh, then handed Valerie five thousand dollars.

"Good lookin' on that info Val, we truly appreciate it fasho... Oh, and do you still dance?"

"Yeah, I still do my thang."

"Okay cool, well maybe I will come break bread with you sometimes and check out yo' work."

"Bet that up baby. I would love for you to come check me out and see that I ain't got all this ass for nothin... So until then, you got my number, use it." *There was a momentary pause between them after her emphasized statement, as Brick briefly imagined himself fuckin' da' shit outta' all of that fat ass.*

She made her ass jiggle extra hard as she made her exit out of the safe house they'd met up at.

--Adolph took a long drag off the cool long as he sat in the shadows a few houses down from the safe house... He smirked to himself when he saw Valerie emerge and climb into her red Honda civic. Then a few moments later, he discreetly pulled off behind her into the night traffic.

One week later:

-As Brick stood in the kitchen at Ray Ray's house assisting Sheila on making some tacos, the news-report that flashed across the screen caught his attention.

"The body of an unidentified man was pulled from the Detroit River yesterday when it was spotted by a River-Sweeper who was in the area collecting debri from the water. Police suspect it was definitely foul-play due to the two bullet wounds to his head, as well as the concrete-filled buckets that entombed both of his feet. Investigators say it was most likely the gases in the victim's stomach that caused the body to swell and float to the surface. —Also, the body of a 26-year-old female-stripper identified as Valerie Gates was found in a wooded area not far from the river that the man's body was pulled from. Police are working to see if the two murders may somehow be connected, but they currently have no suspects in custody and both cases remain open."

"Damn! That muthafucka Adolph got to her." Brick mumbled under his breath as he continued to assist Sheila in preparing dinner.

Chapter 32

Officer Smitty Branch activated his lights on the patrol car, then a few moments later, he cruised to a slow stop behind the gray ford focus he'd just pulled over. It was around eight-thirty PM. And even though the female driver commited no traffic violation, Smitty pulled her over anyway.

As he approached her window, the 28-year-old black woman had her license and registration already in hand.

"You mind telling me why I'm being pulled over tonight officer?" She asked respectfully.

"As a matter of fact, I can. You failed to put on a signal back there when you turned off Gratiot to conners." He told a bold-face lie.

"With all due respect officer, I did not fail to put on a signal, and I'm not calling you a liar. I'm just saying you must have my car mistaken with someone else's."

"No no no sweetheart, I don't make mistakes. So just sit tight and I'll be right back after I run your information." He patted the roof twice, then strolled back to his patrol car... The woman sighed somberly as the reality of the bullshit set in. She then became a little more uneasy when she realized they were in a somewhat secluded location with not many motorists passing by.

Officer Smitty approached her car a few moments later with a ticket in hand. He handed her the credentials back, then said-

"I got some good news and some bad news." She displayed a shocked expression before he continued.

"The bad news is your vehicle insurance is expired and I'm gonna have to impound your car. The good news is, we can work somethin' out if you wanna pull off as if we never met." The woman's heart started beating rapidly in her chest, and she was truly afraid to ask him what he had in mind, but she did.

"What did you have in mind officer?" She spoke nervously... He opened her door so he could be shielded, then stepped closer to her and said-

"Well, when I pull my dick out, I want you to see how fast you can make it skeet-off with that pretty mouth of yours. Then you can be on your merry way."

The woman was flabbergasted, appauled, and scared to death from what the monsterous-looking bad cop had just purposed. She could hardly control her trembling hands as she mumbled-

"I have a baby in the car sir." Officer Smitty shined his flashlight in the backseat and smirked when he saw the opproximately three-year old baby-girl asleep, strapped in the car-seat.

"She look sleep to me. So depending on how good the head is, you can be done before she wake up." *He ended his statement with a matter-of-fact expression on his face...* At this point, the woman was truly outdone. She'd heard about shit like this happening in the hood, but never in a million years thought she'd ever be a victim. She thought about how badly she needed her car for work and day-care. And reflected on how complicated things would be for her if her car was taken tonight... So she took a deep breath, said a silent prayer, and promised herself she'd try everything in her power to correct it later. A quiet tear strolled down her chocolate face as she submitted to officer Smitty's gross violation...

Smitty placed one hand on the door, and the other on the roof. He closed his eyes momentarily as he felt the pleasurable sensations from her warm, wet mouth engulfing portions of his member.

"Oh shit, that's what I'm talkin' 'bout baby. I knew you was good. I could tell by your lips." He mumbled as he engrossed himself in the moment, then reached down and palmed the back of her head, holding her steady as he pushed more of himself deeper into her throat... He continued to grip her head as he began to hunch his hips forward with a quickened pace. He would get more excited when he noticed her gag from time to time, and it only caused him to hunch much harder.

Spit consistently dripped from both sides of her stretched mouth as the session grew more intense by the second. Officer Smitty now had both of his hands firmly gripping the back of her head. And he knew that within a matter of about eight-seconds, her mouth would be over-flowing with his semen... Suddenly, the baby cried out,

"Ma- Ma." And Smitty could feel the woman instantly try to retreat as she slightly turned her head in her baby's direction, but Smitty gripped her head harder, then abruptly re-adjusted his dick in her mouth so he wouldn't lose the momentum that had him on the brink of the payload... And after another four seconds in her head, his body convulsed aggressively as he ejaculated in her mouth. He firmly held her head in place until the very last trickle came out. He took a deep breath, then zipped his pants up and mumbled,

"Okay mam, enjoy the rest of your night." Then he casually walked back to his squad car. He smirked when he noticed the baby staring at her mother as he walked off. And he was fully aware of the fact that she probably witnessed the last six seconds of the act.

He climbed in the car and thought to himself,

"Fuck it if the lil bitch saw her mama getting' some action. Now she'a know what to do wit' a dick when she grow up. Ha ha ha." He laughed at his own foul thoughts as he pulled off into traffic and faded into the night.

Chapter 33

Chop's breathing grew heavy as he continued to punch the heavy bag at the Downtown Boxing gym. He had been training for four years, but he only used the sport as a form of therapy now... Chop was well on his way to becoming a pro fighter before the run-in he had with a crooked Michigan State Trooper. The traffic-stop for a cracked taillight turned violent when the rogue officers tased him repeatedly, beat him mercilessly, then put a false case of *assault on a police officer* on him that never happened. Chop was on probation for a gun-charge at the time, which caused the courts to send him back up-state for five years. That's when he met Brick.

After making it home and taking a shower, he browsed through the assortment of designer clothes that occupied his closet. He decided on wearing a white long-sleeved burberry button-up. Paired with some burberry blue jeans, complimented with some white airforce-one-boots. Chop brushed his one-against-the-grain fade, then slid on a pair of burberry transition-frames, a heavy black leather coat, then casually slid out the door... As he headed down the service-drive towards the freeway, he reflected on one of the reasons he was fully loyal to Brick. *When Brick got out of prison before him, he stayed true to his word. He took care of Chop's two sons, and his mother. And also made it a point to send Chop money until he got out. So in that regard, he couldn't see himself keeping any secrets from Brick for Adolph. So he immediately put Brick up on Adolph's side-hustle with the heroin.*

As Chop continued on his trip to take his children some shoes and money, he noticed the overhead lights from a Michigan State trooper's car directly in his rearview, which instantly caused a flood of bad memories to bombard his mind. He prayed that things would be different this time as he came to a slow stop. But just as the thought kicked in, all he heard was −

"Step out of the car, now." Chop took a deep breath in an effort to remain calm before responding.

"Why is that officer. If I commited a traffic violation, can you please just give me the ticket so I can make it to my kids."

The Caucasian trooper aggressively opened the driver-side door as the tall black trooper approached the passenger-side.

"Listen gottdamit, I'm giving you a direct order. So step the fuck out of the vehicle now!" He demanded.

Anger grew inside Chop as the foul-mouth state trooper spoke with more provocation. And at this point, he felt that he already knew the officer's intent...

The black officer made his way around to the driver-side and positioned himself beside the aggressive Caucasian.

Chop took another deep breath, then put his hands up and stepped out of the car...

The foul-mouth trooper instantly began patting him down in a rough manner, then out of the blue he yelled-

"Stop resisting! Stop resisting!" as he slammed Chop to the ground.

Chop couldn't believe that the same corrupt shit was about to happen again... The black trooper instantly joined in yelling-

"Show me your hands! Show me your hands!" as the other officer pushed, punched, and shifted his body in an effort to make it look like Chop was resisting.

The Caucasian trooper pulled out his taser and sparked it against Chop's back... Chop yelled out in pain, then immediately wrestled his way out of their grip... The moment he made it to his feet, he instinctively side-stepped the rushing black trooper and landed a vicious left hook to his chin that instantly put him to sleep. Then he focused his attention on the Caucasian trooper.

The trooper suddenly found himself cornered against the squad car. Trapped, confused, and hurt as Chop delivered a barrage of lethal punches to him. The trooper tried to fight back but it was uneffective as Chop delivered more of the brutal punishment to his face.

The trooper instinctively went for his gun but was swiftly dropped with a looping overhand right. Chop picked up the dropped taser off the ground, then pressed it against the trooper's red neck.

"Aaaaaaaaaaaaaaaaaaggghhh!

"Aaaaaaaaaaaggggghhhhhh!!

The trooper yelled out in agonizing pain as Chop pulled the taser off, then re-applied it to other parts of his body.

"You like that bitch! Huh! This how you like it bitch! You low life piece'a shit!" Chop continued to tase him until the battery had lost an effective charge.

185

Loyalty Ain't Loyal Enough

Chop delivered a final hard kick to the trooper's bloody head, then jumped in his car and screeched off into traffic, headed to drop off the money to his kids on the chilly November day.

Chapter 34

As Brick stood in the high-end jewelry store, he peered in the mirror to see how good the new Cartier glasses looked on him that he was about to purchase. He turned toward his female cop friend Linda and asked-

"How they look baby?" She flashed a bright smile before answering.

"They look perfect baby."

"In that case, I'll take'em." He slapped seven thousand on the counter and walked out with them.

Later on that evening:

Brick and Linda sat in the parking lot of a gentlemen's club on eight-mile and Dequinder, waiting for a dude name Al to come out.

"He should be out any minute baby, cause he picks his lady up around this time every Thursday, Friday, and Saturday like clock-work."

"Okay." Said Brick as he reminisced about the favor Linda asked of him in return for the favors, she did for him.

...As Al emerged from the strip-joint with his lady, Brick abruptly pulled down the ski-mask and put the carty's on. He got out the car and ran up to them in a hurry...

The moment he entered their space, he placed the forty caliber glock to Al's forehead.

"Shut the fuck up bitch!" He yelled out just as Al's lady was about to scream. Then he spoke directly to Al.

"Nigga these Carty's cold as hell, ain't they?" Al didn't answer. He just stood there dumbfounded as Brick continued to quiz him.

"Whassup nigga, you don't fuck wit' Buffs nomoe. I heard you dat dude that be goin' around poppin' lil seventeen-year-old niggas fo'em. So why you ain't getting' excited now? I'll tell you what dawg, since you so fucked up about carty's, Imma' lace you with these. But you only get to sport these bitches under the dirt you hoe-ass-nigga!" Boca! Boca! Boca! –Boca! Boca! Boca! Boca!

Brick purposely avoided shooting him in the face. He took the carty's off and placed them on the face of Al's dead body, then abruptly focused on his girl as she stood there froze and scared to death.

"Ay bitch! You betta' make sure that nigga have them carty's on his face at the funeral, or I'm comin' for yo' bitch-ass next!"

Brick made a quick stride back to the car, and Linda made a low-key swift exit out the parking lot into traffic... Linda was so turned on by the move, that she sucked on his dick all the way to their destination.

Al had robbed and killed Linda's 17-year-old nephew on his prom night for some cartier glasses that his father let him sport that night. Everybody in the area knew who did it, even law enforcement. But they could never get enough evidence to make it stick. So Linda took matters in her own hands... Now they were even. Linda went to the funeral a week later, and sure enough, the carty's was on his face.

****

The second that Officer Smitty Branch appeared on the block, the three black teenagers that sat on a porch, instantly tensed-up and began to complain.

"Damn dawg, there go Freddie Kruger ugly ass. And I know he on some bullshit." The youngsta' named Corey spoke up because he normally had the most problems with him.

"Yall know the drill muthafucka's. Get da' fuck against the car, now." Smitty demanded... They all complied.

He searched the other two boys first, then when he began to search Corey, his 16-year-old sister Ashley came out the house and asked-

"What's goin' on officer, what did they do?" Officer Branch ignored her as he continued to pat Corey down... He then made a foul statement to Corey as he patted down his left side. Corey's left leg was replaced with a prostetic leg do to a bad car accident he had two-years prior.

"You still one-step-pimpin' nigga? Huh? Corey tensed up as the words pierced his feelings, but he took a deep breath and didn't react.

"Did you hear me officer. What did they do?" Corey's younger sister asked again.

Officer Branch looked back at her with a threatening look on his face before responding.

"You keep talking Ms. thang and you gettin' a pat-down next."

"What the fuck ever!" She spat back as she stormed in the house, slamming the screen door.

Officer Branch snickered at her, then leaned closer to Corey's ear.

"That lil' hot pussy ready fasho, what you think bro?" Corey instantly lost his cool and spent around with quickness.

"You betta' watch yo' muthafuckin' mouth dude, foreal!" Officer Smitty released a sinister chuckle before he swiftly kneed Corey in his stomach, then aggressively slammed him to the concrete pavement as hard as he could. He stomped his head against the concrete several times, then reached down and abruptly snatched his prostetic leg off... He savagely began beating Corey all over his body with the leg. Corey yelled out in pain over and over.

"Okay man. Okay! Aaahhhggg! Help me. Somebody help me!" Corey's forty-eight-year-old neighbor came running out of his house up to Corey and the officer.

"Whoa Whoa Whoa officer. That's enough man. He's got the point."

Seconds later, the neighbor abruptly threw his hands up and yelled.

"Okay sir! Okay, I'm sorry I interfered!" He quickly turned around and darted back into his home as officer Smitty kept the trained weapon pointed at him after yelling-

"If you take one step closer muthafucka! Or let another word come out them dick-suckers, Imma' plug yo' bitch-ass and get away with it. Are we understood muthafucka!"

Officer Branch focused his attention back on Corey, then delivered at least five more blows to his head and body with the prostetic leg. He stood over Corey breathing heavily, as he laid curled-up on the ground writhing in pain. Smitty popped the trunk, tossed the prostetic leg inside, then slammed it shut. He began mouthing off a few more words to Corey before he pulled off.

"You lucky you ain't goin' to jail for assault on a police officer, you fuckin' clown."

****

When Chop pulled up on the mother of his kid's block, he swiftly pulled over in the black camero and got out when he noticed her walking up the street... He caught up to her in a few quick strides, and he could tell from her expression that she was happy to see him.   He smiled at her, then seized the opportunity to feel her softness as his rough hands groped her plump ass aggressively.

"Hey babe, whassup, where you headed?" He asked curiously.

"I was just walking to the store to grab some cigarellos for my blunts later."

"That's whassup. Where my boys at?"

"They at the house."

"Okay, cool. Imma' stop down there and holla at'em before I go. I was just fallin' thru to drop off the new retro's I grabbed for them, and some change for yall. So here you go." He handed her two-thousand dollars.

"Thanks baby, we truly appreciate all that you do for us. And they truly appreciate having a damn good father. And I'm sure you already know that I feel blessed to have you as a friend, if nothing else." *There was a momentary pause between them as he reflected on losing a good woman like Adreena because he couldn't get out the streets... He looked her over from head to toe and silently sighed at how good she was looking in the pink Lambskin jacket, the pink fitted Nike sweatsuit, with a pair of pink stiletto boots to match.*

"You should really spend some time with me in a room tonight. I need to bang dat thang out nine-one-one."

"Why is that babe, that sound like a stress-call. You alright, whassup?"

"Yeah I'm good, just got a lot on my mind right now. And you seem to never fail at makin' shit all better."

"Well check this out babe, I was supposed to work tonight, but I can call in 'cause it was just overtime. So I'm down for linkin' up with you later, fasho."

"Bet dat up Dree, that's what I'm talkin' 'bout baby... Oh yeah, you know you gon' still be my wife one day."

"Yeah right nigga, promises promises. Yo' ass just happy I said yes to some pussy." They both laughed simultaneously.

"Oh yeah, I almost forgot to tell you. Your oldest son Mr. Martez wanted to call you yesterday to tell you about the little boy he knocked down with a straight-right during their sparring session last week. Now he can tell you in person." Chop smiled before responding.

"That's my boy. My future world champ, fasho."

Chapter 35

As inmate Dawhite Walker emerged from the shower in Ionia State prison, a lone black middle-aged inmate rushed into his space wielding a homemade knife. The man didn't waste any time poking his body savagely as Dawhite attempted to block the forceful strikes with little success. The knife penetrated Dawhite's head, face, neck, chest, back, and stomach. The man mumbled in Dawhite's ear as he continued to push his knife.

"This for killin the baby of a boss, nigga!" Dawhite screamed out in pain as he fell to the floor, with his assailant landing on top of him. The convict had no mercy as he continued to stab Dawhite in a callous fashion, aiming for all the vital areas of his body... Suddenly, someone yelled out,

"C/O!" as the three correctional officers came running full speed towards the attack. By the time they were in full view of the two inmates, all they witnessed was a bloody man on top of another man yelling out

"Help! Somebody help him! He's dying!" then the convict performed several chest compressions on Dawhite, and immediately began giving him mouth to mouth breaths, appearing to make an effort to recessitate him... Unfortunately for the convict, the officers didn't fall for it. They tackled him down, then handcuffed him. Then they rushed Dawhite to the prison hospital where he later died from his wounds. He was stabbed over thirty times by a lifer who had nothing to lose with the system, but a lot to gain from the underworld. He was paid fifty-thousand dollars for the hit.

****

State Attorney Mrs. Drew twirled an ink pen in her left hand as she spoke on the phone with a Caucasian male judge from the Wayne County District.

"Judge Picket, I would truly appreciate it if you can expedite the warrant for officer Branch sir. Reason being, he has been re-instated as an officer for less than six months. And it would be an under-statement sir to say that he is egregiously out of control. There is currently eight pending lawsuits against him as we speak for things that should be unthinkable for a man with a badge. I felt that it was a mistake when he was reinstated and feel that it would be an even bigger mistake to preserve his position. I want him off the streets now your honor."

A few moments later Mrs. Drew smiled as she heard the words

"Enough said." Then focused on the signed warrant coming through the fax machine.

Chapter 36

By the time officer Branch made it to the precinct, he felt as if his heart skipped a beat when he overheard a few detectives talking about the fact that there wasn't a body found in the house that recently exploded in the Boston Edison District. He wondered to himself *'What could've possibly went wrong.'* And it was very unsettling to him. He felt that he was somewhat back to square one as he reflected back to the way he got the location of Ray Ray's main house before the feds did. *He knew that the feds would do two months on and one month off with their method of surveillance on Sheila's parents' house. So he did his own surveillance during the month that the feds were off of it and caught a lucky break. He pulled Brick over a couple blocks away after he'd left their house. And even though he didn't know for sure whether or not he was affiliated with Ray Ray, he decided to take a chance on looking into it anyway... Brick never even noticed the small magnetic tracking-device Smitty placed under the back bumper of the Yukon he was driving. And when it finally paid off, Smitty never told the feds about it because he didn't want Ray Ray in prison... He wanted him dead.*

Officer Smitty Branch finished up some paperwork, then left out the station a short time afterwards. He stopped at McDonald's and ordered a big mac, large fries and a mountain dew. By the time he made it about two blocks away from the Mickey D's, a black full-sized van abruptly pulled in front of his squad-car, blocking him off. - Four men jumped out with high-powered weapons drawn, and didn't waste any time snatching him from the car, aggressively forcing him into the van. Brick and Adolph were two of the assailants, and Adolph cracked jokes about how many different ways they should kill him, all the way to the fifty-acre piece of land that Teko owned in Adrian Michigan. -----

Sixty minutes later when they'd finally arrived, they positioned officer Branch next to the large wood-chipper that sat in a densely wooded area of the property. Then left him there for about thirty minutes alone. When they did return, officer Smitty's nerves were instantly rattled the moment he laid eyes on Ray Ray.

"Ay Ray Ray my man, what is this shit all about?" Ray Ray smirked at him before responding. Then calmly said-

"I'm 'bout to show you." He signaled for Brick and Adolph to let the games begin. And the eagerness in Adolph showed immediately as he threw a hard, wild punch, instantly breaking his nose. Then he hocked up a disgusting glob of spit, and offensively discharged it in his face.

"You piec'a shit! If I had time I would fuck you dude. The same way I use to fuck all corrupt pigs in da' joint the very second I found out who they was. Dat boy-pussy was mine. And I know you wanna' see my dick, don't you bitch. Yall faggot-ass cops always curious about a nigga dick. Coward muthafucka!"

Brick laughed at Adolph's anxiousness to violate Smitty, and he shook his head shamefully before speaking up.

"Dawg, I ain't even gon' follow up my nigga's play, 'cause what you about to experience gon' trump anything I coulda' thought about doin' to yo' hoe-ass."

Brick grabbed him and shoved him inside the hoist, then maneuvered it until he had officer Branch placed directly above the wood-chipper. Officer Branch instantly began to plead for his life and cry hysterically as he watched himself being lowered toward the razor-sharp twirling blades of the menacing machine.

Suddenly, officer Branch began screaming to the top of his lungs as his toes and feet were grinded up and shooting out of the exit portion of the machine in tiny pieces. Brick allowed the grinding to continue until he got to his waist, then stopped it. Officer Smitty was still alive and was somehow still able to beg for his life... Brick used the paused moment to share a thought with Smitty.

"Dawg, I just wanted to see the look on yo' ugly ass face before I turned yo' ass into hamburger meat. And I also wanted to say, yo' dumb ass couldn't even blow a muhfucka up right you dummy. Oh, and here's the tracking-device you put on my truck you clown." He stuffed it in Smitty's mouth with aggression.

"Okay, that's all. Now die screamin' like the coward they trained you to be." Brick hit the button on the machine again, and they all watched stoically as the rest of his body was lowered into it. It truly amazed them to watch him disappear in such a brutal fashion as his neck and head was the last thing to fade into tiny pieces of flesh-n-bone. When it was finally over, Ray Ray casually walked over to them. - Boh! Boh!

"Aahhhgg!" The two quick slugs to each of Adolph's kneecaps caused him to yell out in pain as he dropped to the ground.

"What da' fuck man! What da' fuck you do that for nigga!" Adolph shouted.

Ray Ray stood over him nonchalantly before responding.

"I think you already know the answer to that, dawg." Brick didn't hesitate to use the same contraption he'd used on Smitty to hoist him up and get him in position over the wood-chipper.

"Dawg, let me ask you a question." Brick spoke to Adolph as he scratched the side of his head.

"Why was you lettin' yo' biological mama suck yo' dick?" Adolph instantly began laughing at Brick's question before answering.

"Nigga fuck dat' crack-head bitch. That triflin' hoe use to suck niggas dicks with the bedroom door open. I even watched the bitch suck two muhfucka's off at the same time. One nigga had about a ten-and-a-half-inch dick, and the other chump had about a twelve. And the bitch made each one of them lames shit completely disappear in her muthafuckin head. And everytime the bitch did it, she knew I was watchin. So after awhile I said fuck it, the bitch might as well get her coke from me. And I might as well get some of dat' good-ass head from her. That's the fuck why, ol' nosey-ass nigga!"   Brick appreciated the explanation, but still felt that he was a fucked-up individual in the head... And he also appreciated the fact that Adolph continued to make threats of revenge as they lowered his body into the wood-chipper.

"Fuck yall bitch-ass niggas. I'mma see yall bitches in hell, and it's on nigga! You hear me!...Aaaaaaaaahhhhhhhgggggg! Aaaaaaahhhhhgggggg! Aaaaahhhhhhggggg!" ----- Suddenly the screams stopped. And all that could be heard was the noise from the running machine.

A grim chapter in Ray Ray's life was over. Now it was time to focus on his new position.

****

Location. Detroit, Mi.
FBI Headquarters: Debriefing

"Okay ladies and gentlemen, this is an update on the fugitive-status of suspected gang-leader Raynard Thompson, a-k-a Ray Ray, and his wife Sheila Thompson. We now have reason to believe that they are frequently returning to the metro Detroit area, for reasons unknown at this time. But as a result of this intel, we are ramping up our efforts to put pressure on anybody in the community who may be assisting them in their efforts to remain elusive. In the event that we come across these individuals, I want you all to keep in mind that they are more-than-likely in possession of military-grade munitions. They have a high propensity for violence. And have a callous disregard for human life. Our felony-warrants are still active, and I will see you all back here in this office sixty-days from today for another briefing... Which will basically be based on any new information that may arise between now and then. So until then, be safe out their special agents, and happy hunting."

As the Caucasian special agent ended the session, he sipped from a cup of coffee and stared intently at the photos of Ray Ray and Sheila on a profile board with a worry-some expression as he mumbled to himself,

"What's next for you muthafuckers. What should I be anticipating?"

Chapter 37

As Myonly and Love attentively sat in front of their computer's focused on the days lesson from their Spanish teacher, the sound of the doorbell caused Love to turn towards one of the security-monitors momentarily. Then she calmly ran to the back patio-area to Ray Ray.

"Daddy, uncle Brick is at the door."

"Okay baby, I got it from here. Thanks for bein' on point."

"You're welcome daddy."

After Ray Ray let Brick in, Brick casually handed Ray Ray a cellphone that belonged to a man named Eddie, who swore his allegiance to Mr. Alverez forever. There were 35 names in his contacts who also pledged their allegiance to Mr. Alverez. They all refused to recognize the transfer of power and vowed to conduct business the way Mr. Alverez did. They also let it publicly be known that they would never take orders from Ray Ray, nor turn over any of their drug profits to him under no circumstances. Ray Ray instantly reflected to a quote that his wife shared with him from a man named Nicolli Makevelli.

"War can never be avoided. It can only be postponed." Brick had already assassinated Eddie, so he listened patiently as Ray Ray gave him a new set of orders to be carried out.

"I want everybody that's listed in that phone, hit. But before you hit them, I want you to place a (*sound good*) contract on each one of their mother's-on-Mother's Day, got it?"

"Fasho." Brick answered calmly over the digital money-counter that Sheila was operating at the table, as she counted small mountains of money and converted them into large, neat stacks.

Brick was now a key member in Ray Ray's organization. He assisted in the day-to-day operations of several cities in the Midwest, cities on the East Coast, and several cities on the West Coast.

A (Sound-Good) contract was a coded-term they used for murder.

****

As time went forward, Ray Ray was still receiving valuable information from his new organization. He was given a variety of different contacts inside several police precincts. And was instantly informed on the status of every player in all the cities that he controlled, who were willing to pay for dealer-protection, and pay the mandatory street-tax to his organization. He suddenly had more tentacles than an octopus. And every one of them was touching something vital.

Ray Ray allowed himself to be re-invented on a level that would be hard to mimick from those who would eventually come behind him. *He raised the muthafuckin bar with this move. And was now considered a boss of all bosses...*

He only had to eliminate 17 dudes in Eddie's contacts before the rest of them fell in line. And he didn't have to carry out the (*sound good*) contracts on their mothers either.

2 weeks later:

An internal problem arose inside the organization that caused Ray Ray to call for a mandatory meeting in Chicago to meet with three more of the top cartel members of his organization. One of the men was trying to veto a (*sound good*) contract that Ray Ray wanted carried out on one of the workers under their umbrella. And Ray Ray was well aware of the fact that voting against this one could possibly gain him a new line of powerful enemies. So he knew that he had to strategize the situation to afford himself leverage whenever he'd meet with the other bosses. Which is why it was obligatory to talk to Teko before he could ever step foot in a meeting with them.

Bitter-cold temperatures gripped the city and several vehicles were stalled through-out the area. Ray Ray laughed at how uncomfortable Teko was, driving in the sometimes-brutal Michigan weather. – They parked outside of a starbuck's, then went inside to have the discussion over coffee and cappuchino.

"I truly love the Eastern Market around this time of the year my friend."

"Why is that Teko?"

"Because they bring in the freshest seafood from all over the world." Ray Ray nodded a casual approval in agreement with the statement, then took a few sips from his cappuchino.

"Okay my friend, as for the business at hand. When you meet with these individuals, you must never, at any point display any form of weakness."

Ray Ray interjected.

"Because any weakness can be exploited." Teko smiled before continuing.

"Yes, that is correct my friend. And I'm proud to see that you've gotten yourself acquainted with our little sacred black book, because that is always a bonus when you are on this level of our game. Now, like a wise man name Patrick once told me, we must compare our way of life to the game of chess, because the rules basically apply the same... He explains it as such. *The average player only knows his next 1 to 3 moves, so he or she would be considered an amateur... A pro will know the next 4 to 5 moves... A master will know the next 6 to 10 moves. And a grand master will know the next 11 to 15 moves.* Be a grand master my friend, because every man in that room will undoubtedly be 3 out of 3 things. *Greedy, Ambitious, and Ruthless.* So with that being said, I'll leave you with one of my most valued pieces of information, which came from a man named Mark Twain. *'Never let your schooling get in the way of your education."*

Chapter 38

Ray Ray scanned the room with an aura of noble vigor, making direct eye-contact with every cartel-member in attendance before he spoke.

"Gentlemen, the reason we are having this meeting today, is because Mr. Gomez went against business-protocol. He gave his crew permission to infiltrate five counties in West Virginia that were under the control of a man name Chulo, who's officially insulated under my establishment. In the process of Mr. Gomez moving in on his territory, three of Chulo's top lieutenants were assassinated, and large amounts of currency was taken. Chulo has always played by the rules, his lunch-money is always right, and once again, he was still solidly under all of our protection when this gross violation occurred. That's why I feel that this order should (*Sound Good*) to all of you as well." As Ray Ray concluded, one of the three men in the room spoke-up in an agitated tone.

"Ray Ray, you sound over-eager in your aspirations my friend. Which compels me to remind you that despite how you may feel, it is against our rules to allow you to commission the murder of that man. So, there will absolutely be no unsanctioned hits on our watch. I'm sure Mr. Gomez had a logical reason for making a move like that. And besides, he's very-much still under our protection as well."

Ray Ray cleared his throat, then quickly rebutted in a stern voice.

"According to our sacred book-of-rules, page 33, second paragraph, not anymore." No-one said a word for a few lingered seconds, then Ray Ray spoke up again.

"Gentlemen, a famous gangster once stated, 'It's not titles that honor men, it's men that honor titles.' And under the oath that we took when we were initiated into this organization, the statute clearly states, the title of loyalty supercede's any allotment of loyalty that's not considered loyal enough." The room fell deafeningly silent again for a few seconds before one of the men spoke-up.

"So how do you suggest we approach the order of business that you propose?" Ray Ray spoke-up matter-of-factly.

"Neutralize the threat, take control of all of his assets, and give Chulo back his territory. Gomez owns several pieces of real-estate in a few different states. But his most prized possession resides in Playa Mexico. It's an ocean-view property, half-a-block from fifth ave, half-a-block from the beach. There are 30 units in total in the complex. And each unit is worth a half-a-mil apiece. Each man in this room will automatically own a piece of it, once the business-at-hand is carried out. Without putting up one red cent, due to the nature of his violation."

There was a shot-glass filled with Bacardi-rum that sat in front of each man. And they carried out the session just like the gangsters that came before them did. Each man that was in favor of the (*Sound Good*) contract, downed the rum, then placed the glass up-side down on the table in front of himself... Two out of the three men had empty upside-down glasses in front of them. And Ray Ray instantly knew that the third man named Scarzo who opposed the hit, would someday be a problem for him... But for now, he silently thought to himself *"Fuck dude."* Because the contract was officially about to be carried out. And Ray Ray currently held more power than him. So in that regard, it was what it was. —Gomez was hit two weeks later, and Chulo was granted his territory back.

Loyalty Ain't Loyal Enough

Yvonne sipped a cup of coffee and reflected back on the day that she sat among a room full of politicians and dignitaries, as she concluded her presentation on residential and commercial development in the inner-city of Detroit. She was ecstatic when she received the news that she was qualified for the grant to put her vision to work. It was one of the most exciting times in her life. She only wished her son Smoke, and her fiancé Rob was there to witness how she brought it all into fruition. It was her new recreational Center that was built in the heart of the ghetto, called the HOOD DRIVEN CENTER... The first thing you noticed upon entry was a big, illuminated sign that read *'Positive Attitudes.' If you believe you can, you can:* Then you walk into a place that was based on enhancing your mind, body, and soul in every way. It taught you how to give respect and be respected. It provided mentors that were experienced in everything from academics, to baseball, basketball, boxing, and much more. They offered free computer courses, free breakfast, and free lunch as well. It was a state-of-the-art facility, and absolutely no nonsense was tolerated. It was one of Yvonne's most prevalent accomplishments... She could've easily got Ray Ray to fund the project, but according to her, she didn't want a single dollar of *blood money* involved in it. Knowing it would always

213

be vulnerable to possibly being compromised. And in that respect, Ray Ray fell back and let her make it happen with the government's money, *the real blood money...* Nevertheless, he was more than proud of her accomplishment. And remained on standbye in case she would need assistance at some point in the future.

Yvonne had a town-hall style meeting on opening day. In which all residents of the community were welcome. The mayor, chief of police, and other authoritive figures were also in attendance. And a hot meal for everyone that attended, was scheduled to be served after Yvonne's hour-long speech.

45 minutes into Yvonne's speech:

"Young people, our communities are literally warzones. And they are building prisons faster than they are building recreation centers... I lost my fiance' a few years ago, as well as my son to street violence. And there's not a day that goes by that I don't feel portions of the pain that came with those losses. Yet I power on like my future husband would've wanted me too. He was actually an ex-gang member, who changed his life and became an activist for young men and young women who looked just like him. He loved the work he was doing, and truly wanted to see positive changes impact our communities in the most effective ways. He wanted to stop the school-to-

prison pipeline. And summon lawmakers to put a concentrated effort into job training, economic growth, and programs that reflect a minorities' self-worth. He wanted to root-out minority-exclusion when it comes to grant-money for small businesses, and stop the incarceration rates from soaring, even when crime-rates in impoverished communities are down... Ladies, gentlemen, and young people. My fiancé passed the baton, now this is my life's work. I owe it to him, my son, and most importantly myself. I believe every race of people should be included in the forward-progress of our great nation. But I especially want a particular race of people to stop feeling like they are disposable whenever they look in the mirror and see a black man or women staring back... This recreation center is just one piece of our economic survival plan. And I promise you all this, as God is my witness, every member will be treated no less than family. Because that is what we are, family. Now let's get Hood Driven for the right reasons yall. All praises due to the Most High." There was a standing ovation with heavy applauds as she concluded.

****

The unmarked car that occupied two narcotic officers, drove by the dope-house on Canton and

Mack at a slow speed… The line of dope-fiends that was wrapped around the corner waiting to purchase the heroin that recently killed five people, caused the two Caucasian detectives to shake their heads in disbelief. There was officially an active investigation on those responsible for the packs of heroin that was labeled *Deathrow*. It was nothing like law enforcement had ever seen. Not only was it a high-grade in purity, it was laced with a known horse tranquilizer combined with the deadly drug fentynol… A massive raid on the five spots where they knew it was actively being sold, was scheduled to be executed in two days. The only name on all of the warrants was *"Crack-head Anne."*

When Chop got Anne settled into the new safe house, he instructed her on the new order of business. She was to immediately stop cutting the dope the way Adolph had her cutting it, and cut it to where it was *'still a top dog without killing customers…* He also instructed her to change the name of it from *Deathrow,* to *Teflon.* And made it clear that she was to never again show-up at none of Aolph's old spots again under no circumstances. She knew her son Adolph was missing but was non-the-wiser of him being assassinated. Ray Ray was also Chop's new supplier of the heroin. And as long as

Chop agreed to never cop outside of their organization, he had Ray Ray and Brick's blessings all across the board... Chop opened up a boxing gym shortly afterwards near downtown Detroit called *KNUCKLE-UP BOXING*... And Ray Ray and Sheila also invested in his vision and promised to eventually have one in every major city.

Chapter 39

Sheila casually walked up behind Ray Ray and lightly tapped him on the shoulder as he stared through the glass-doors watching Myonly and Love play gracefully in the huge backyard of one of their many homes. The weather was beautiful in Miami this day, and nothing meant more to Ray Ray than to see his wife and children happy... Sheila hugged him snuggly from behind, then gently placed something in his right hand... When Ray Ray looked down and reviewed the object, he abruptly spun around and looked at her with a surprised expression before speaking up.

"Are you serious baby?" Sheila responded with a bright smile as Ray Ray processed the positive pregnancy test she'd just shared with him.

"Yes I am my king. You are gonna be a proud father of another one of Allah's beautiful blessings... And we are going to name him- "

"Whoa! Whoa! Whoa! –baby whatchu mean him." Ray Ray cut her off emphatically.

"Like I said my love, him."

Ray Ray scratched the side of his head in a puzzled manner before responding.

"Baby ain't it too early to tell things like that?"

"Yes, but I just got an overwhelming feeling that it's a boy this time. And I already got a name for him."

"Am I gon' like it?" Ray Ray asked skeptically.

"I don't know, but you should like it."

"Okay, tell me what it is."

"It's Izreal."

"Israel. You mean like the country Israel?"

"Yes, only spelled differently. I-Z-R-E-A-L, Izreal because he Is-Real like his daddy."

"Okay okay, I gotta' admit, I'm fuckin' wit' it. That's whassup. But check this out, did you cover all bases and come-up with a female-name just in case you're wrong about the boy?"

"Yes I did. And her name would be Serenity."

"Okay okay, I'm diggin' that one too." Ray Ray was floored, and he was more than overjoyed. He called Myonly and Love in the house to share the good news, then called Brick afterwards and shared the good news with him as well.

"I'll be damned." Said Ray Ray to himself as he layed in his bed, enthralled in his private thoughts.

"Izreal or Serenity. Wow."

Several federal agents sat around with heavy anticipation as they finally got the break they'd been waiting for... They were extremely anxious as they felt themselves getting closer than they've been in a very long time to getting their hands on the high-profile suspect whom they considered one of the most dangerous men in America...

...After eight rings, Ray Ray answered his cellphone when he noticed it was Oeekwa calling. He hadn't heard from her since they'd buried his son. And even though he appreciated all of the care she provided for lil Ray outside of his presence, he still had planned on cutting ties with her forever... He'd hesitated on answering the phone because he still wrestled with the fact that lil Ray died in her care. But in the same breath, he felt that he couldn't truly blame her. Because the way he lived his life, Karma was consistently on standbye... So he had to basically charge any of his personal losses to the game. And besides that, Oeekwa was one of the people who helped him find the dude responsible.

"Hello." Ray Ray answered dryly.

"Hey Ray Ray, whuddup doe."

"Shit, whuddup."

"I haven't heard from you in a minute, and I was just calling to see how you was holding up."

---Long pause.

"Hello." Oeekwa spoke up.

-Pause still lingered.

"Hello, Ray Ray, you there?"

Click!- Phone abruptly goes dead.

After a heavy, disappointed sigh. Oeekwa turned towards the many federal agents that occupied her living-room and relayed-

"He hung up."

"Call him back, now!" yelled one of the agents frantically.

-riiiiiiiiiiinng, riiiiiiiiiiinng, riiiiiiiiiinngg,- She called his phone back several times with no success on getting an answer.

Ray Ray had learned quite a few things since he'd been heavy in the streets most of his life. And one of the key things he learned was, if you didn't talk on the phone for over three-minutes, the feds couldn't pen-point your location. And aside from that, he had a built-in scrambling system installed in his phone from one of Brick's old contacts. His phone would bounce from fifty different locations at the top of every hour, then start back over once it got to the fiftieth location. And the best part about it was, he'd never be at none of the locations. He loved it... He didn't know for sure or not if Oeekwa had finally got pressured into giving him up to the feds or not. But he knew that the phone call didn't feel right. And decided to ride with his instincts and never answer another phone call from her again.

Syann had finally persuaded Oeekwa to work with the feds on capturing Ray Ray, because they promised Syann they would cut her time significantly. And she felt that if Ray Ray was in prison, at least she'd have access to him. So her twisted thoughts caused her to break bad. And she constantly told herself that she'd stop at nothing to get back next to Ray Ray, even if it meant losing her life.

The feds were extremely disappointed about the miss, yet they still prepared to ramp-up their efforts to apprehend him one-way or another.

The cartel member known as Scarzo, sat stoically in a room with two other high-ranking members from their dangerous organization. They all puffed on fine cigars as they ended their discussion with a photo of Ray Ray resting crookedly in the center of the polished oak table. Every man had an upside-down glass of empty rum in front of him, so the order to eliminate Ray Ray was now official. They shook hands and gave short embraces, as they smiled and prepared to leave. Scarzo had a personal dislike for Ray Ray, so he placed an expedited order on the hit, which meant it would be carried out within seven days... They violated commission rules by not informing Teko about the contract on Ray Ray, but Scarzo didn't care. And he knew that if Teko ever found out about it, it would be an all-out war amongst the powerful figures.

Epilogue

Sheila was right about the baby... It was a boy, and they did name him Izreal. The feds decided to put Sheila and Ray Ray on America's Most Wanted. And continued to pursue them aggressively whenever a tip came in related to their whereabouts.

The cartel members who voted to have Ray Ray assassinated failed to get it done in seven days. But they still had an active team of assassins in play, who was still in search of Ray Ray around the clock.

Ray Ray eventually amassed over a billion dollars from his underworld ventures. And currently remains one of the largest drug-suppliers in America. And for those who grew up around him, he is known as one of the most Hood Driven individuals that the hood ever produced.

When Teko finally received a phone-call from a cartel-member about the unsanctioned hit on Ray Ray, the first thing the caller said was- "*We got a major problem!"* Shortly afterwards, Teko declared war against Scarzo and the other members involved. –Six months later, authorities were calling their beef one of the bloodiest underworld wars in U.S history... and it was still active at the present time.

Six months later:
As Scarzo emerged from the Italian restaurant in downtown Detroit, a 1300 Habussa motorcycle abruptly pulled up in front of him. Ray Ray lifted the visor on his helmet, then squawked

"Game over for you Scarzo." Boca! Boca! Boca! Boca! Boca! Boca! Boca! He casually blended into traffic after pumping seven bullets into Scarzo's face and neck.

****

One month later:
Five ruthless blood gangbangers from L.A touched down at Metro-Airport in Romulus Michigan, headed to Detroit with one mission on their minds... Finding Raynard Thompson, a-k-a, Ray Ray. During the ride to Detroit, one of the ruthless gang members focused intently on a photo he had in his phone of Yvonne, and mumbled-

"If we find this bitch blood, we find ol'boy. Either way, somebody definitely gon' pay for Damu... Facts."

ACKNOWLEDGEMENTS

First off, I wanna thank the Most High for continuously staying present in my life. I wanna thank my wife and my production team for assisting in bringing this fire-literature to all my supporters. And shout out to all the people who patiently waited for the third installment of this spellbinding four-part series. I told yall it would be worth the wait... Shout out to every platform that I advertised on, much love and appreciation to yall for that. And to all my family and day-one supporters, I love yall wholeheartedly. Thanks again for all your support. Shout out to everybody who's in the fight against police brutality. And shout out to everybody who's chasing their dreams. I'll be coming with some more heat for yall real soon, so look forward to it my literary family. And to my lovely wife, thank you sweetheart for your focused drive in keeping our company strong. I'm forever grateful for all the sacrifices you make and have made to see us bubble. Now in the words of my eight-year-old daughter, stay strong, stay safe, and stay brave.

ABOUT THE AUTHOR

Derek Mack, a-k-a D-Mack was raised by his grandmother on the east side of Detroit Michigan. He is personally in tune with most of the harsh realities that jump from the pages of his crime novels and is certified as being True to the Game by those who played in his circle.

D-Mack is an avid reader and was inspired to pursue a writing career from authors such as, Iceberg Slim, Sister Souljah, Charles Avery Harris and many more. He is currently hard at work creating new material and has a real passion for the literary world. He say's that he is most at peace whenever he's writing stories, sharing his craft with those who enjoy genuine creativity.

www.ingramcontent.com/pod-product-compliance
Lightning Source LLC
Chambersburg PA
CBHW071151260626
47162CB00003B/1001